Pra...

THE THINGS I KNOW BEST

Other Books by Lynne Hinton

FRIENDSHIP CAKE

Coming Soon in Hardcover

GARDEN OF FAITH

LYNNE HINTON

THE THINGS I KNOW BEST

HarperTorch
An Imprint of HarperCollins*Publishers*

HARPERTORCH
An Imprint of HarperCollins*Publishers*
10 East 53rd Street
New York, New York 10022-5299

Copyright © 2001 by Lynne Hinton
Excerpt from *Garden of Faith* copyright © 2002 by Lynne Hinton
ISBN: 0-06-104101-7

First HarperTorch paperback printing: March 2002
First HarperCollins hardcover printing: June 2001

HarperCollins ®, HarperTorch™, and ❦™ are trademarks of Harper-Collins Publishers Inc.

Printed in the United States of America

Visit HarperTorch on the World Wide Web at www.harpercollins.com

10 9 8 7 6 5 4 3 2 1

For Laura Lynne Bender
In honor of your eighteenth year

Acknowledgments

Once upon a time there was a storyteller who
desired to tell her stories. She was not strong
or beautiful or brilliant; and she was hesitant
at first. She was not quite sure of her voice, the
validity of her words, or the merit of the
things she wished to say. So she hid her stories
for a very long time. But then one day when
the sun was shining at just the right angle and
the sky was clear and wide and the air was
cool and expectant, the storyteller, surprising
even herself, said yes. Yes, I will tell my stories. Carefully, she sought wise counsel.
Prayerfully, she searched for those who would
guide her. And first, God sent her grace. And

then God showed her the way. And finally, God gave her light.

A trinity of confidence, three messengers of God, three strong and beautiful and brilliant women lovingly and tenderly called forth her voice, sanctioned her words, and affirmed the things the storyteller longed to say. They bathed her stories in blessing. And the storyteller and the three heralds of wisdom lived happily ever after, brazen, noisy, and fierce.

Thank you to Sally McMillan for your deep and abiding grace, Joann Davis for knowing the way and leading me on it, and Kathi Goldmark for your bright and illuminating light. I am forever grateful.

Contents

The Things I Know Best

1

The Face of Knowing

❧ Tiny pieces of myself floated to the top of the glass, and I began to read my future in tea leaves. Mama and the preacher in the cabin by Sandy Creek, Liddy standing at the Trailways station near a bus going to Atlanta, Mr. Jenkins and the cut of his small, dark eyes, and some union of colors I don't yet recognize. Scrap by scrap, they all danced along the lip like memories in the wake of death. As they brooded and twitched, I stared down into my tomorrow wondering if I should drink from the cup or run to the sink and pour it out.

Reading hands is my sister's means of Knowing. Tiny crooked lines leading up and down, front to back, thumb to wrist, these are the roads she travels. Her fingers hot on your skin, she'll close her eyes, go all blind-looking, her lips counting marks, measuring curves and stops. She can give you the first letter of your lover's last name and open up the secrets of your heart. She's been touching palms since she was a little girl, understanding the life and death that people clutch in their fists in the name of love. By the time she turned nine, everybody in town knew she had the gift.

In spite of our recognizing it at such an early age, though, nobody treated her any more special than they did me. In our family, Knowing is a common sense; and even before I was sure like today that I had it, I knew stuff. All of the women have some form of it. Grandma Pinot interprets the sky, predicts weather patterns, upcoming anomalies, drought, that sort of thing.

Aunt Doris reads dreams and can tell a pregnant woman the sex of her unborn child. Great-grandmother Lodie could heal troublesome ailments and call out evil spirits from the sick and cursed. And her mother before her, Big Lucille, was known to associate with ghosts.

All of the Ivy women have a little something extra that causes the people in town to have a healthy suspicion of our family. So the fact that I now see snatches of another day's events in my afternoon drink isn't frightening or alien; it merely establishes my gift in the parade of women who birthed me and brought me up.

Aunt Doris asked me when I was thirteen and had just started my period if I'd had any special dreams on the night before I'd seen blood. I thought back to what I'd dreamed: I remembered the softness of the ocean, the too-white tips of the waves; I saw myself swimming beneath the rocks and craggy coral with only one long, deep breath, felt a soft-finned dolphin rubbing against my thigh. But I didn't find it unusual enough to mention, since I'd had the dream twice before—both times marking some girlish passage. I shook my head no.

"Never you mind," she said, a cigarette balanced on her bottom lip. "You will Know best."

I suppose it would seem to any ordinary person that Knowing would make the women in our family rich or smart or at the very least well respected; but the truth is the Knowing hasn't given us anything extra. It seems, in fact, to have created a curse. All the Ivy women lean towards making bad decisions, especially when it comes to money and men. And just as we have accepted the ways we all Know, we also have accepted each other's poor choices in husbands and fathers for our children.

Daddy left when me and Liddy turned seven. Grandma came in the kitchen talking about the windstorm that was coming up while Liddy and Mama and me sat around the table watching the candles burn into the cake.

"JayDee left," Mama said, the words all square and neat. Then she blew out our candles. All fourteen of them in one quick, heavy breath. Liddy looked into her hands like she should have known, mad that she hadn't blown first. I just stuck my fingers into the side of the cake and pulled out the thickest pink rose.

I still remember the sweetness of the icing as it

slid down my throat, and my mama's one lone tear snaking down her face.

"He ain't worth your water, Bertie," Grandma said as she reached into her pocket and pulled out a handkerchief. Handing it over, she added, "He had bad blood."

Mama's Knowing has a little more prestige than that of the others. She's the only one in the family who actually makes money from her gift. She foresees death. She gets an uneasy feeling that has something to do with the chirping of bats, that high-pitched way they fly around in the darkness; and somehow an image forms before her and she feels the slipping away of somebody's life, a beat stolen from her chest.

Mr. Lynch, from the funeral home, gives Mama a monthly allowance for her Knowing about death's arrival because he believes it gives them an edge on the planning of work schedules. By knowing in advance that funeral services will be needed, he can decide who can take a vacation and how many extra men are needed to work. He also knows who to call about delinquent monthly installments on prearranged plans. So Mr. Lynch feels it's well worth the hundred and fifty extra dollars a month he pays to Mama, on top of her regular wages. She also answers the phone and fills out insurance forms for him—tasks that are part of her job as the receptionist at the funeral home.

She's been working there for as long as I can remember; and the only death she's missed was the infant daughter of Janine Butler, who certainly wasn't meant to die.

Janine and Russell had gone on a vacation to Asheville in the fall five years ago. Nobody, not even Mama, knew that a bear would steal a baby. They searched the woods and campsites, valleys and mountains, but never found the child. Russell came back to Pleasant Cross to clean out the house and settle his debts, but Janine never came home. To this day people say she walks unafraid into the caves of bears, opening the mouths of lions and pole cats, mountain after mountain, looking for her baby girl.

I asked Mama if she believed that Little Etty was still alive since there was never any sign about the death; but she said the baby's last breath had been so still and tiny that it hadn't attracted the senses of the bats or the stirring within her heart.

Secretly, I've always believed that Little Etty Butler is not dead and is being raised by a clan of bears in the Blue Ridge Mountains. She's growing like a cub, climbing trees, catching fish with her hands, running through the meadow fast and free, her thoughts and memories of a human life dissolved into the dreams of a strong black bear.

Since there was no funeral for the little girl, no arrangements to be made, Mama's pay wasn't affected by this incident.

Liddy and me are now eighteen, just finished General Lee High School and looking for which way to go. Liddy says she wants to head up north, try to make it in beauty school somewhere, grow a window-box garden, and find the boy who's meant for her, one whose last name begins with an *O*.

I haven't got such high ambition, never have. I feel comfortable being around people and things that are familiar. Mama and Aunt Doris agree that Liddy has the streak of desire and I have the stretch of satisfaction. It's true. I'm content not to know anything about tomorrow and to taste the sugar off birthday cakes even in the midst of personal tragedy.

Luther Shepherd, who owns Shepherd's Grill, offered me a job as a waitress serving breakfast and lunch. That seemed good enough for me. And it was here at the Grill, after today's shift, that I discovered the future, slippery in a glass of old tea, and began to worry about what would pass.

Liddy going to Atlanta—the first image my tea revealed—makes me sad and uneasy since we've never been separated. And yet it isn't like we didn't know she'd be going. She almost quit school at sixteen to take a job in Detroit she'd heard about from the guidance counselor. She had train schedules to New York and Washington; and she was thinking about riding up to Boston with Leo Jacobs, who drove a truck up there every other Thursday.

She's been planning to leave for as long as we've been sisters, so it comes as no surprise that the time is at hand. At least Atlanta isn't as far away as New York or Boston.

Mama and the preacher, Reverend Lawson— now seeing *them* together in my glass is a little unnerving, even though I've seen the way he looks at her during altar calls. His forehead gets all sweaty when she walks down the aisle, and he holds her tighter than the others when she stands before him confessing some sin she can never seem to get shed of.

Whenever I ask her what it is she's done that she has to go down front every Sunday, she just shakes her head and looks far away into some past trouble that she won't name.

The preacher's wife doesn't like Mama much and never speaks when she comes to the funeral home with her husband. She gives us all the iceberg shoulder and a look down her nose that makes me think maybe she's Lutheran or Presbyterian and doesn't really want to be with the Baptists. Mama isn't too bothered by it, though;

she says there's only one thing worse than a carousing, sex-starved preacher, and that's a married one.

The signs of this future event have been around for a long time too. So even though I know it will get her into a mess at the church, maybe even cost her her job, even that image doesn't cause me too much worry.

It's the look on Mr. Jenkins's face. The tightness of his breath. The mean curl of his lip as he cuts his eyes away from my Knowing image. This is the piece that stays on me. This and the arrival of some remnants of color I feel pleasure from but can't describe. Herein lies the predicament that I detect isn't all goodness.

Mr. Jenkins runs the savings and loan on the edge of downtown. He also owns just about everything and everybody in Pleasant Cross. His daddy, Olaf Jenkins, didn't trust banks and wouldn't set foot in one; so when the Great Depression hit and everybody lost their money— he had a nice stash in his barn that he loaned to people at a considerable interest.

When they couldn't pay him back, he took

possession of their farms, their houses, and any land they owned. Somebody said he even took a pet pig away from Curtis Murray when Mr. Murray couldn't pay back his debt and the house he lived in was rented. Took the pig and cooked it, stabbed it right in front of Mr. Murray's house while little Curtis stood on the porch and watched. Grandma says that's why Curtis is a railroad drunk today.

Mr. Olaf Jenkins had a surly reputation; and his sons, Donald and Tyrus, didn't fall far from the family tree. Donald died young many years ago when a tractor he'd repossessed for his father fell on top of him, getting, as all the folks say, what he deserved. Tyrus Jenkins, the banker, the one in my tea glass, is known to turn down loans to anybody he doesn't approve of, and that's about everybody in town. He's the mayor and the chair of the town council, and everybody owes him something.

So you see, he's not a man to dream of or think much about; and he's *certainly* not a person you want to see floating in the pictures of your future.

"You ready to go home?" Liddy, who has a job over at Tina's House of Beauty, has covered her eyelids with eye shadow. She bats her long black lashes at me. "It's Silk Lapis. Do you think I look like a rock singer?"

She's just the same as me, long-armed and skinny, clumsy feet, sharp bones, and a thin oval face. Only she wears a lot more makeup, colors her hair, and shops at the mall.

"You look like you rubbed Easter eggs all over your eyes." I say this as I yank off my Shepherd's Grill apron and throw it in the basket of dirty linens by the trash can.

Luther, taking a breather during the after-lunch lull, pulls a toothpick from his mouth and peeks up over the afternoon newspaper. "Tessa Lucille, don't forget you got to refill the ketchup bottles first thing in the morning."

"Yeah," I answer.

"Why does he call you all that?" Liddy whispers. She erases the date and the special of the day off the chalkboard before we leave and writes, "Today is the fist day of the rest of your life." (Spelling wasn't her best subject in school,

14

and she rarely looks over what she's done.)

I shrug in answer to her question and decide not to correct the error. I grab my jacket off the coat tree, knowing that it's way too hot to wear it now but remembering that it'll be cold at five-thirty tomorrow morning, even though it's summer.

Liddy is happy. I can tell by the way she's walking. Light and airy like the ballerina in our homeroom. We always tried to walk like Elizabeth Hines. She had blond hair that she tied up in a tight bun, and she never seemed to look down. She wasn't so very tall, but it always felt as if she was a head above everybody else. She carried herself like she was the daughter of royalty. We'd practice at home with a book on our heads or a roll of paper towels under our chins, hoping to look like her. But we were never able to walk with that kind of pride and instead just looked like we were trying to show off our breasts.

Elizabeth got a scholarship to the School of the Arts and left early in the spring to travel up north before her college began. There was something about her being real smart that they let her leave two months before high school was over. Or maybe it was that the art school didn't care if she had a diploma or not; they were just worried that her knees might get damaged in PE.

Anyway, looking at Liddy now, I think that maybe she practiced when I wasn't around, because she seems so tall and righteous.

"I'm going to Albuquerque," she says suddenly, stopping and turning right towards me, her chest high and puffed out. "That's in New Mexico."

"I know where it is," I say. And I'm unsure now if maybe I misread the leaf with Liddy's life on it. Maybe I mixed up the towns that start with *A*. "What's in New Mexico?"

"Tina's cousin's family." Liddy is looking at herself in Clifford's Used Bookstore window. She's rubbing the blue up to her brow and shaping it with a finger that she licked for just that purpose.

"Liddy, you don't even like Tina. What makes you think you're going to want to stay with her cousins?"

❦

"First off," she says, turning around, her eyes like two drops of water—clean ocean water that won't spill—"I never said that I didn't like Tina. I just said that she should have never dyed her hair that burgundy color and that she really didn't have a flair for fashion. And second, I won't be staying with her cousins that long— just until I can find a place of my own."

"Here." Liddy licks her finger again, takes a swoop of Silk Lapis from her right lid, and smears it on mine.

I roll back my head and close my eyes as she paints me. When I look up and see ourselves in the window, we're the same. Only each outside eye is shaded in blue. We're one big woman with arms and legs on the inside that we don't need.

"When are you going?"

"Sometime in July, maybe August. I'm going to do nails at Tina's during the day and cashier at Cordessa's every night but Monday. I can work two shifts on Friday and Saturday." Liddy turns to walk back up the street towards the funeral home.

"I figure in eight weeks I can save about fifteen hundred bucks. That should get me going in Albuquerque." She's about ten steps ahead of me.

"Cordessa's?" I ask, hurrying to get beside her. "Cordessa's? Have you told Mama?" I wipe the sweat off my forehead. I can't believe what I'm hearing.

"I'll tell her tonight." Her tone is firm, but her shoulders aren't quite as tall as they were in front of the bookstore.

I look at her in disbelief.

She looks back, sort of haughty-like. "Tessa, we're eighteen now. Mama can't tell us what to do anymore."

We stop at the intersection, then turn in the direction of the funeral home.

"Being eighteen don't mean anything to Mama when it comes to Cordessa," I say. We cross another street and head into Mr. Lynch's parking lot.

Liddy doesn't say anything back to this because she knows it's true. Mama has some sort of weird disposition towards Cordessa Pender.

The most I can put together is that Mama and
Cordessa were best friends growing up. In spite
of the fact that Mama is white and Cordessa is
black, they were always thicker than thieves and
closer than sisters. That's what Aunt Doris says.
They were even almost related, since Aunt
Doris's son, our cousin Jasper, was living with
Cordessa's daughter, Millie, before she died in
that train wreck in Florida.

Millie's death was a sad and shocking event
for the family. And Mama wouldn't go to the funeral, even though she knew about it before
everybody else since she heard the bats and then
saw Cordessa walk by the funeral home with a
cloud passing over.

I remember that church day as a time of in-
tense negotiations between Mama and Doris.
Aunt Doris claimed that Mama owed it to the
family to be there in support of Jasper and that
she needed to let the past be healed. Mama just
turned to her sister and told her in that real
quiet, serious voice that she'd better leave.

That's when I first heard about the "incident"
between Mama and her growing up friend.

Liddy and I asked Grandma while she was outside checking the skies with her wet finger pointed to heaven what had happened so many years ago that Mama couldn't forgive. Grandma wouldn't say much except that Cordessa and Mama had lost themselves in some storm that nobody had foreseen or understood. And that some things were just meant to be left unknown.

She said it like she'd rehearsed this answer, repeated it so many times, to herself I guess, that she'd finally come to accept it.

Mama dropped out of school and went to work at Lynch's, although she'd been planning to go to the nursing college in Greensboro. I guess she packaged up her pain and inability to move beyond Pleasant Cross, North Carolina, and labeled it Cordessa Pender.

It appears that even though Mama wears sadness like a second skin and seems to be always trying to rid herself of it, she's going to stay covered if getting free means she has to fix things with Cordessa.

Cordessa graduated, they say, and married Max years and years ago but apparently left him after she bought the bar on the interstate. Mr. Pender still lives in their house back behind the tire plant. He was at Millie's funeral sitting with Cordessa, quiet and limp, moving like an old dog trying to find a place to rest. Aunt Doris had the family over to her house after, since everyone knew it was awkward to be at Mr. Pender's and nobody thought a bar would be a good place for a funeral gathering.

I remember Mr. Pender standing in the corner of Aunt Doris's kitchen. Jasper and Cordessa were huddled up in the living room, smoking cigarettes and playing in their plates of food. Everybody was gathered around them trying to attend to their needs. But Mr. Pender just stood in the corner, his big black hands in the pockets of his too-small brown church suit. One of his shoes was untied. His hair had been combed and greased in the front, but the back looked like he'd been standing up against a wall all night. He was the saddest person I'd ever seen because he didn't have a way to bring his grief inside of him. It just sat on his shoulders and clung to his arms and chest like a hand-me-down sweater, heavy and old. He couldn't seem to find a way to smooth it down or take it off. The loss of first his marriage and now his beloved child had covered over his heart.

Mama took some cat-head biscuits and red-eye gravy, a gallon of tea, and some plastic silverware over to Aunt Doris's while everyone else was at the service. But she didn't go to the church, nor did she go by the east end of the trailer park while Cordessa was there. Even now, all these years later, she's sort of like a fox having seen a fallen chicken feather when it comes to Cordessa: she won't let it loose.

When Liddy and I walk into the funeral home I'm once again reminded of the smell of death. It's hollow and old and spiced up with formaldehyde and a strong perfumed lotion. Sometimes it's still on Mama when she comes home, and it drifts from her clothes and skin and lands on the surface of my tongue, coating my supper. This time, since I know we're having pork chops tonight, I clamp down my jaws and decide not to speak.

Mama is shuffling through her papers and gives us a nod to go over and sit in the big wing-backed chairs that are right beside the door. Mr. Lynch is in the Viewing Room, and I hear a woman crying, though it's very soft.

A man speaks from behind the closed door. "Your mother had beautiful skin. I hardly had to add any blush." Mr. Lynch isn't known for his ability to comfort.

The woman sniffs and I hear a tissue being pulled from a box.

"I'll leave you alone with your beloved," he says. "You take all the time you need."

But I know he doesn't mean it. Mr. Lynch likes to have his lunch at one-thirty. It's almost four-thirty, and I know he hasn't eaten. It's Wednesday, and Mr. Lynch always comes to the Grill on Wednesdays. The special is chicken pie.

He comes out of the room and closes the double doors together with his back to me and Liddy. I look over to her and we smile at each other because he doesn't even see us. He walks on over to Mama.

"I'm going to get some crackers and a Coke, Bertie. Can you stay until Miss DuVall is finished?"

Mama just rolls her eyes and plops herself back in the chair. She had already gathered up her purse and magazine.

"Thank you, Bertie," Mr. Lynch says, turning towards the back of the office.

"Liddy, run up to the IGA and get some potatoes," Mama says, opening up her wallet and pulling out a bill. "Here's five dollars." She holds it up while Liddy walks towards her.

"Why don't you ask your other daughter to go?" Liddy asks, not thrilled with her assignment.

"Because she's been standing all day and you've been sitting. I figure you need the exercise. Besides, Tessa makes the best potatoes, so she'll be cooking them."

Liddy breathes out a puff of air, takes the money, and walks out the door without looking at me.

"You make any tips?" The phone rings and Mama answers before I can tell her that I got only about eight bucks after serving breakfast and lunch.

Without Mr. Lynch and the truckers, I don't make much money on Wednesdays. But I was glad I didn't have to speak since I was determined not to let the funeral home mess up my supper.

It's Aunt Doris on the phone, and Mama starts arguing about satellite movies and the phone bill. I get up and walk to the big double doors to the Viewing Room. One of them has drifted open and I want to close it, figuring that giving the bereaved her privacy is the polite thing to do.

Miss DuVall is talking out loud. As I get close I can make out the words.

"I know I didn't always do right by you, Mama. Not as a child and not now." There's a pause.

"You never did like Buddy, and you didn't hold the baby long enough to see how much she looks like you."

I stand and listen even though I know I should shut the door and sit back down.

"It wasn't easy being your daughter, always knowing you didn't approve. Always waiting for that look you handed down like a sentence. That look of wishing I was somebody else's child."

I peek through the crack. Miss DuVall is stroking the dead woman's hair. She looks like a little girl with a doll.

"You know what, though, Mama? I don't need anything from you anymore. Not your approval. Not your understanding. Not even your love." She takes another tissue.

"I wanted all those things so bad for so long that I tried everything I knew to feel some little piece of your satisfaction. I know now that I can do without. There's other love that feeds me, better love. Little Katie—even with your eyes, she looks at me like I've done just fine."

Now she straightens her hair.

"So you go on to wherever it is you're going. Heaven or hell. I don't care. It doesn't matter to me who you're lounging with. I don't have to pull my chair up near you again."

Liddy comes back into the funeral home and

🌿

closes the door forcefully, startling me so much that I slam the double door I'm holding. I throw my mouth wide open—and before I know what's happened, death has slipped across my lips.

"You want white potatoes or red?" Liddy is talking to me and Mama both, but Mama tips the receiver beneath her chin, hand over the mouthpiece, and answers, "Red. They cook better, don't they, Tessa?"

"Yes, ma'am," I say, fully aware that talking won't bring about anything worse than what's already happened.

Liddy turns around, grunts at Mama, and pulls the door shut behind her.

Mama is still talking to Aunt Doris. I move back to the wing-backed chair, my heart still racing from the shock of Liddy's entrance. I pick up the *Southern Life* magazine that's sitting on the table beside me and flip through the pages, looking at pictures that seem nothing like the southern life I know.

Big white houses with wrap-around porches and broad-leaf ferns in lovely rope baskets. Little blond, freckle-faced children in crisp seer-sucker suits playing on long green lawns. Large fruit pies with gentle slits on top that have just enough fruit dripping out to let you know that the filling is hot and rich and sweet, sitting on front-yard picnic tables with lace cloths and big crystal pitchers of lemonade.

I know that there are people who live that kind of southern life—even people in my own town—but most of the folks I know and grew up around would have a different set of pictures to share than what this magazine sports.

There'd be front porches, but they'd have stacks of newspaper in brown bags on one end and the old living-room sofa on the other. Children would be playing in the front yard—a patch of red clay probably, and maybe an old oak tree—but they wouldn't be in matching suits; they'd be in stained T-shirts and droopy diapers. There might be a picnic table and even some fruit pies, but don't nobody I know put real cotton cloths outside. We use the heavy plastic ones that fade in the sun, the kind you get from the grocery store, or paper mats that have a map of the United States.

Flipping through these pages makes me wonder if *Southern Life* magazine might ought to change its name to *Rich Southern Life*.

I'm looking for another magazine when Miss DuVall comes out the door and looks my way. She's red-eyed and petite; and I remember her from a few years ago at the county fair, where she sold cones of french fries from a booth outside the car show. She was only a few years older than me and Liddy, but I remember thinking how grown-up and lucky she looked behind that counter with all that free food.

Now she looks childlike and broken, but I know from her talk to her dead mama that she's not torn-up and splintered. She's a woman who's finally on her way. She nods at me and walks out the door.

Mama hangs up the phone, hollers out to Mr. Lynch, who's come back from the store, and together we walk out behind the grieving daughter. Liddy is just on her way back from the IGA, so we get in the car with Mama driving and me in the back; and I watch Miss DuVall pull the rearview mirror towards her face, adjust her makeup, lift up her chin, and drive forward. She turns briskly out of the parking lot, having already said her good-byes.

I don't think to tell either Mama or Liddy about Miss Duvall's conversation or the future I saw only a few hours earlier. I figure it will come to them as it needs to. Besides, I'm waiting to hear how Liddy will inform Mama about her New Mexico plan and about how Cordessa Pender is helping to finance her travels. This will prove to be more exciting than any speculation about Mr. Jenkins or gossip about a dead woman's daughter.

We ride along listening to the country station, no one talking. The windows are open since Mama doesn't like the air-conditioning, so the wind whistles through the car. With that noise and the music, we wouldn't be able to hear one another anyway.

I'm looking at the back of the heads of the women I'm most like. Mama is chewing gum.

And even though I can't see her from the front, I can tell that she's enjoying the taste of spearmint as she rolls that gum around in her mouth.

Mama is smaller than me and Liddy, takes more after her daddy than the Ivy side of the family. She's a good foot shorter than the two of us, and seemed a little sad when we shot up past her when we turned fourteen. She carries herself like a bigger woman, though—walks tall and can yell like a man.

Her older sister, Doris, is wiry like Grandma and wears tight Wrangler jeans and soft, thin blouses with elastic around the top so that she can pull them down over her shoulders. She's small-waisted and has an iron-flat butt. She likes to go to the Cowboy Club and dance in those lines of people. And just like Mama is always chewing gum, Doris loves to smoke.

Mama holds her fingers straight up as she drives, the steering wheel in her palms. Her nails have on their second coat of Sinful Scarlet, but you can't tell from where I'm sitting. Liddy painted them Sunday night and touched them up again this morning, and now, even at the end of the day, they look like they've just been done.

The late-afternoon sun is lowering and children are out on bikes and in back yards jumping on trampolines. It's a peaceful time, an easy time, because summer has finally allowed kids the freedom that was stolen from them by the order and schedule of school.

We drive past the old hatchery and Hasty's Store. We hurry by old farmhouses and gardens that stand young and tenuous. Because the soybeans, corn, and tobacco haven't reached full maturity yet, you can still see back behind the fields where the pine trees are tall and the woods are thick with late-spring growth.

We drive past the turnoff to the lake and the first entrance into the trailer park. We do this since there's a fifteen-mile-per-hour speed limit and speed bumps every thirty feet. We've found over the years that it's faster to go in the second entrance, head towards the back of the park, and go in on Dillon Street.

We're in the family home near the northwest corner of the Ivy League Trailer Park. Doris and Deedle, Mama's younger brother, and the other family members all live in trailers closer to the other end of the park. That's more towards the first entrance.

It was just farmland around the old home-place until Doris's ex-husband, Lester Garron, found a way to have most of the land deeded over to him. Then he sold it to Tyrus Jenkins's realty company to turn it into a trailer park. Aunt Doris and Deedle, who signed all their land away, both thought Lester was just finding out how much the land was worth and needed their signatures for permission. Imagine their surprise when the Jenkins bulldozer drove up and pushed over their barn and chicken houses.

Deedle stood at the door of his little shanty with a shotgun and blasted out the headlights of the dozer, but it didn't matter. Lester had been real careful to make sure everything was legal and binding before he cashed his check and headed to Florida.

Doris and Deedle didn't have anything to do but go to a portion of Grandma's part of the land that sided up to the last lot at the front portion of the park. They bought trailers with the rest of the park tenants and moved back like strangers onto the land that had been in the Ivy family for over a hundred years. The only thing anybody in the family got from the sale of the land was the name of the park, Ivy League, something Lester must have thought was a real treasure.

Grandma Pinot and Granddaddy Jacob, who died when me and Liddy were twelve, built the house she lives in now. And Mama and JayDee moved into the old Ivy house when they first got married. Mama never left. And except for a brief stay at Grandma's when Mama had a bad spell with her nerves, that's where I've always lived.

Jasper lives in a trailer right next to his mother, Aunt Doris. And Uncle Ray, Grandma's brother, lives in the one next to him. He's what everybody calls a hermit; we don't see him except on Sundays and holidays. I don't know what all he can do in that little trailer all day and all night, but Doris says he's got some strange ways and more than sixteen cats.

Granddaddy Jacob's sister, Claudette, lives one space down from Ray; and two second cousins from our granddaddy's side, Fay and

Wanda Gayle, live next to her. We don't see them much since they aren't Ivys, but we still regard them as family.

So you see, even though Tyrus Jenkins owns most of the land that used to be ours, the Ivys and our relations have managed to wind ourselves right on the outskirts of town and wrap around the back half of his holdings. I suppose that provides a little comfort to those who have died and are still watching.

When I get into the house, Liddy has already walked back to her bedroom, planning to take off her work clothes and put on her shorts, I presume. I go into the kitchen and start peeling the potatoes that Liddy left on the counter. I don't care about changing clothes since I'm used to being around food while in the uniform from the Grill. Besides, I have three of these gold dresses, so I don't have to wash one out every night.

Mama gets the pork chops out of the refrigerator and turns on the TV to watch the news. Liddy comes back into the room and goes over to the pantry to pull out a jar of beets from last year's garden; then she looks in the cabinet for a box of cornbread mix.

We're like some old married couple, the three of us, having learned our routines—even created our own habits—based on the patterns of each other. It's the way we do things, like a family of worker bees, each one satisfied to have a useful job—one that was assigned to us but that would have been picked by us anyway because it suits us right.

We know, for instance, with regards to fixing a meal, that Mama is best with the meat. She just knows how to cut it and baste it and how long to let it cook in the grease. She breads the chicken with a special mixture of potato chips and garlic and tenderizes the pork with Chinese sauces. And she can pick out which cuts will go the farthest. When she was little she used to care for the animals on the farm, and I guess it just became second nature for her to know, by feeling, which piece of beef or which slab of pork is going to be most satisfying.

I'm best with the staples—the potatoes or beans, the rice and collards. I've discovered that

I have a knack for seasoning them that makes them taste almost as good as Grandma Pinot's. And she's definitely the best cook in the family. I've always liked gardening and have learned that knowing how to cook leafy vegetables begins in the dirt. You've got to know how much lime to put in the soil to keep the leaves green and tender and how to prevent rot with strips of old newspapers tilled in the dirt. I know that you've got to cook them slow and without much stirring since you don't want the flavor to get lost in the juice.

I'm in charge of the potatoes now because I learned that if you peel them and roll them in butter and salt before you boil them, they'll mash a little easier and give a fuller flavor. I'll also pull out the leftover green beans from Sunday and put them on the stove with a tiny cooked piece from Mama's chops. With that and a pinch of sugar, I know they'll be just as good as they were the first time.

Liddy knows the garnishing. She gives each plate color and knows just what relish or chow-chow to set on the table to accent the vegetables

I've prepared. She knows tonight, for instance, that the purple in the beets will create an appetizing array with the white potatoes and the brown pork. She knows that sour pickles or hot peppers are best with pinto beans and that bread-and-butters or corn relish tastes better with greens. She looks around at what Mama and I are working with and goes right to the pantry or the refrigerator and pulls out the perfect side dish.

She also bakes the biggest, softest biscuits and the best cornbread in the Ivy family. And Liddy, like Grandma Pinot, is known for her iced tea. She even sold it while she was in high school and made enough money to go on the band trip to Disney World. She and Grandma claim it's so good because they stick a finger in it, to give it some natural sweetness; but I don't know about that.

I've noticed that this division of labor in the kitchen works the same way when Mama and Doris start cooking over at Grandma's. They just seem to know what has to be done, what everybody expects, and what their task is. This comfortable cooking structure is a familiar and tasty part of Ivy life.

I look over to Liddy to see if her eyes will reveal how she plans to let Mama know about her fancy summer itinerary. But she just looks away so she won't have to think about it. The pork chops are popping and the potatoes are boiling, so we know that supper isn't far off.

I leave the kitchen to change my clothes, and that's when I hear the conversation start. Only it's Mama who starts it. She Knows.

"What you doing over at Tina's?"

"Nails and cleaning stuff, same as always." Liddy's voice sounds tight and thin.

"You planning on staying there for the summer?" Mama Knows; no doubt about it, Mama Knows.

I hurry to put on my black running shorts and a T-shirt. I wear the same shirt from yesterday even though it has a great big stain on the bottom. I put my uniform in the hamper and use the bathroom.

"Tina's cousins?" says Mama as I emerge from the bathroom. I've missed maybe two or three exchanges between them. Mama sounds surprised. "What makes you think Tina's cousins want you to come and stay with them?"

I walk back into the kitchen, trying not to act curious or worried. I stir the potatoes and push a small one against the side of the pan to see how soft it is.

"Tina said she'd talk to them. They have a big house with an extra room since their brother joined the Air Force."

The TV news is blaring about a thunderstorm warning for the area, and I wonder if Grandma has already taken in her laundry and put up the chickens.

"Why is New Mexico of any interest to you?" Mama asks.

"I read a book about it in school. Tessa, you remember—I did my social studies paper on it in ninth grade."

Uh-oh, she's looking for help now. I'm being asked to choose sides. I don't care for this predicament, not one bit. I've been here before, and I know it never turns out good. Not for anybody. I nod towards Mama like I know what she's talking about. It's *somewhat* of a commitment to Liddy's side. I certainly don't remember any paper on New Mexico.

"It's a great place for a young single woman. Tina's cousin owns a beauty parlor in town. She says I could start work as soon as I get there." Liddy's mixing the cornbread batter and pouring it in the pan. She's trying to act unconcerned and normal.

"I told you girls that I don't have any money to give you right now. I can't afford to send you out there only to have you turn around and come back." Mama puts the lid on the pork chops.

We're all cramped together in the kitchen, trying to sort through a life, each of us still engaged in our own tasks.

"I don't need any money from you." Liddy holds her breath while she slips between us and puts the cornbread in the oven.

"Liddy, the bus ticket itself is more than a hundred dollars. You've got to eat; you'll be paying rent. How you going to get around out there? You can't pay for yourself with that little bit you get at Tina's."

Standing with her back to our backs, Liddy starts to clean up her mess on the counter. "I got a second job," she says.

With supper almost ready I need to set the table. I get real close to Liddy when I pull out the silverware from the drawer. I look at her with all the devotion I've got. She smiles at me.

Mama doesn't see this since she's still facing the stove. "A second job? What kind of second job you got?"

I get the forks and a spoon, three knives, and the paper napkins and walk from the kitchen into the adjoining dining room. Liddy's on her own.

"Cordessa offered me a job at the bar. I'll work three nights a week, maybe four. I'm going to cashier. I'll get paid by the hour, and the waitresses will give me part of their tips."

Mama doesn't say anything. I can tell she's turning over the pork chops because the popping gets louder. Liddy has braced herself against the countertop.

❋

"That's not going to happen" is all Mama says.

Liddy opens the bottom cabinet and throws the trash in the can. "Oh, yes it *is* going to happen. I start tomorrow night." She closes the cabinet door and turns around to square off.

Liddy and Mama have always had more fights than Mama and me have. Liddy's four minutes older than me and maybe she's just got that older-sibling growniness about her. I don't know. I figure Mama is so tired out by the time she's through with Liddy that I don't have to argue with her about much.

I don't like arguing anyway. Even without a sister, I can't imagine that I'd fight as much as Liddy does. It tires me out, sucks me dry, so I try to avoid it like the stinging nettle at the edge of the woods behind the house. Unlike me, Liddy's fueled by it. And because she's always wanted more from Mama, she's always had more to fight about.

Our life has never been enough for Liddy. Not our clothes or how many nights we could go out or how early we could date or how long we could stay somewhere. Not where we camped when we went to the beach or how many flowers we put in jars or how much makeup she got to wear when she was little. She's always been dissatisfied about *everything*.

"Liddy, I'm not fussing with you about this. You are *not* going to work for Cordessa Gordon."

"It's *Pender*, and what's so wrong with Cordessa Pender? Grandma said you were friends a long time ago. Why do you hate her so much?"

Mama puts down her fork and turns to Liddy. "This is not open for discussion. You are not to step a foot into her establishment. Do you understand me?"

Well, it wasn't much of an argument from Mama's end. There weren't any utensils thrown or doors slammed. Mama wasn't allowing for any discussion. It seems to me like it's an open-and-shut situation. Liddy will have to find somewhere else to work. Maybe the IGA is hiring cashiers for the night shift.

"I'm eighteen years old, Mama! I happen to like Cordessa Pender, and I like the chance to work in her bar. I plan to be there only through the summer; then I'm leaving for Albuquerque. I've made up my mind, and you can't do anything to stop me!"

I look at my sister. Red-faced and confident, she's prepared for war.

"Then I suggest you pack your things right now, because as long as you're living in this house, you're doing what I say. And I say you are not to work at Cordessa's!"

Mama takes the pork chops off the stove and turns off my potatoes. She peeks in the oven at the cornbread, turns off the TV since *Wheel of Fortune* has replaced the news, and walks to her bedroom. I go back into the kitchen and shake my head, trying to signal to Liddy to leave it alone for now. "Let it rest," my eyes tell her. But she won't listen.

She follows Mama to the back of the house. "I'll pack my bags all right! I can live at Grandma's. I'm tired of living in this house anyway. It's an old house filled with ghosts! And you're always in my face about something! I'd be *happy* to move out of here! The sooner the better."

Liddy has threatened to move out every time they've had a fight. This is nothing new for her. Usually Mama ignores her, shrugs her shoulders, and goes on about her business; then Liddy calms down and everything goes back to normal.

But I know this ain't normal.

Mama walks up from her bedroom to Liddy's, which is across the hall from mine. "Fine. I'll help you pack." And she starts pulling Liddy's clothes out of the closet and throwing them on the bed. I can't see what's happening, but I can read the sounds.

I look down the hall and see Liddy standing at the door watching Mama. Her face is a cloud of confusion and a stone of stubbornness. The next thing I know Liddy has run into the room full-force and my mother and sister are fighting.

I race down the hall and look in the bedroom. With clothes flying and hair being pulled, Mama and Liddy look like they're some tag-team wrestling duo that's suddenly turned on each other.

The bed collapses as they bounce onto it and

roll off, pulling the curtains down with them. Liddy's bleeding. I'm not much help at all since they're caught between Liddy's bed and the back wall; I can't separate them. It's just elbows and obscenities. I can't find anything to grab hold of and pull them apart.

Finally Mama stops. She's the one been doing most of the hitting, and I guess she thinks she's made her point. She pushes herself up from the floor, wipes her hands down the front of her pants, touches up her hair, and says, "I expect you out by tomorrow morning." Then she walks out of the bedroom and takes her keys from the table. After a minute I hear the car start. She floors the gas and backs away.

"Holy shit, Liddy!" I drop down on the floor beside her. "What on earth just happened?"

"She hit me in the mouth." Liddy struggles to get up. I help her go over to the mirror and we look at her bleeding lip. "That bitch hit me in the mouth."

"Liddy, you should have let it alone. I told you this thing between Mama and Cordessa is old and deep. I've never seen her this wild."

I comb the back of her hair with my fingers, then fall back on the broken bed. It's real quiet for a minute. Then I sit back up and start straightening stuff. I reach for the curtains and prop them back up. The rod got bent, but it won't be hard to hammer back into the right shape. The spread's dirty, but that can be washed. I don't know what happened to the bed frame. When I begin to put her clothes back in the closet, Liddy stops me.

"I'm not staying here, Tessa, so don't put those dresses back. I'm going to Grandma's." She takes an old T-shirt and wipes the blood off her lip. It's started to swell.

"Liddy, don't."

She talks like I didn't see what just happened.

"Let me get you some ice," I offer, wanting to do *something*. I go into the kitchen and wrap an ice cube in a dishtowel. When I get back to the bedroom, Liddy is sitting on the broken bed. She's a small and crumpled doll.

"It's not a big deal," I say. "She'll get over it. Just find another job is all." I hand her the dish-towel and sit down next to her.

❧

"I don't *want* to get another job." She throws the bloody T-shirt behind her. "I had to beg Cordessa to give me this one."

I look her in the eye. "Had to *beg* her? I thought you said she asked you if you wanted the job."

Liddy touches her lip with the ice and then starts to straighten her hair.

"Well, *begging* is probably too strong. I just went by to see if she had any openings. She didn't want to hire me because of Mama."

"And looking at things now, don't you think she was right?"

Liddy shrugs her shoulders. "It doesn't matter anyway, because I finally convinced her to hire me. And I'm taking that job."

"Liddy, why are you so bull-headed? Why does it have to be Cordessa's? You *knew* it would make Mama mad. What's going on with you?"

Just then I smell something burning. As I jump up from the bed and run towards the kitchen, the smoke alarm starts whistling. Sure enough, the cornbread is burning, smoke rolling from the oven. I pull the pan out but drop it on the floor when my finger grazes the oven rack. I turn off the stove, get the broom to knock off the smoke alarm, and start opening windows and the door.

When I'm finished and look up, Liddy is in front of me with a suitcase in her hand. She's still holding the dishtowel to her lip.

"Damn, this is a mess." That's all she says as she walks to the wide-open door. "I'll come back for my other stuff tomorrow when Mama's at work."

And with that she grabs her flip-flops from by the table and walks out onto the porch, then heads down the path to Grandma's.

2

The Close Patch of Color

❧ The supper plates that me and Mama fix, now that Liddy is gone, are flat and void of color. Most days I try to add a bit of flash or demonstrate some flair with a slice of tomato or a sprig of dillweed, but it just doesn't offer nearly the same flavor as a dish of Liddy's.

We don't talk about work or the gossip I hear from time to time at the Grill or the sales at Wal-Mart anymore either. We just listen to the news, then let the TV stay on for *Wheel of Fortune*. Since she can always guess the puzzle, Mama never thought she'd like the show that Aunt Doris finds so appealing. But the spinning and the power of chance and Vanna's delightful nature seem to satisfy her in a way she hadn't expected.

I see Liddy almost every day. She takes a late lunch and eats with me after my shift. She's been gone from the house two weeks now; but it doesn't seem so different, except for the tired silence at night, the pallid nature of our supper table, and the neglected state of Mama's cuticles.

She's still planning to go to New Mexico by the middle of August. Tina's worked it all out with her cousins so that she can have her own nail booth at the salon as soon as she gets there. While she's waiting and saving, Grandma doesn't make her pay anything for staying at her house. And she gets free food at the Grill since she read Luther's palm a year ago and told him not to marry Christine Cooper. (She didn't see any *C* in his hand.)

He thinks she saved him from a world of sorrow, since after he and Christine broke up her mother moved up from Greenville, South Carolina, and lives with her now. She had a stroke last Christmas and requires round-the-clock care. Christine lost a whole lot of weight since the breakup too, and Luther has never trusted a skinny woman. He likes his women round and curious. Now that Christine is otherwise, he can't figure out what he saw in her.

Liddy keeps trying to get me to come by Cordessa's, says I'd really like the bands that play, but I'm not interested in moving in with Grandma. And I'm confident that would be the general consequence of any such action. It's not so far from us and there are three bedrooms at Grandma's—enough to go around—but I like the big house.

The ghosts Liddy mentioned are harmless. We think there's a baby, a rebellious teenager, and some old man. They mostly stay in the top part of the house, the closed-off section, upstairs where Great-aunt Phyllis used to live; but sometimes they must get bored and slip through the keyhole or under the edge of the door and head downstairs, knocking things over and lighting candles.

We've never really seen them; but everybody in the family claims they're here, restless and stuck in that in-between place betwixt heaven and earth. We fix them plates of food every New

Year's Eve, and whether it's the squirrels or the ghosts, *somebody* eats everything but the butter.

I'm used to the place now, the spirits, the gaspy sounds of settling and release, the leaks, and the bigness and the smallness of our home.

Great-great-grandfather Lewis Jewel, Lucille's husband, built the house; and everybody who comes in finds that it's oddly constructed. Some of the rooms, like the living room and the master bedroom, are enormous. Our furniture looks swallowed up and out of place in them, like a crib and toys in the nursery when the baby's died.

It used to make me afraid to walk from the hallway into these rooms. The walls seemed to pull away from me, and the ceiling loomed and stretched way above, making it seem that I'd entered a completely different reality, some alternate universe where I was locked away from everything familiar. A room, *one* room, closed off from the others, that goes on and on and on.

And then there are the very small rooms, like my bedroom and the hall bathroom. These are so tiny that I can't imagine what Grandfather

Lewis had in mind except maybe very small children who would grow up and out of these rooms and into the big ones at the end of the hall.

But I've found, after living here most of my life, that I'm now accustomed to the uniqueness of the place and find myself attached to its quirkiness. It's become like a member of the family, strange and not always useful, but welcoming and full of my secrets.

I don't even mind that it's terribly hot in the summer without air-conditioning. It can be brutal at dusk in July, when the air is still and the fan is circulating only that warm summer heaviness. And sometimes I wake up at two or three in the morning and I'm wet from the top of my head to the soles of my feet, the bed soaked in my sweat. Sometimes it's almost unbearable; and I feel held down and pressed in by the weight of the humidity.

But often the breezes will be cool and bathed in the sweetness of my roses and the wild jasmine. Now and then they'll drift through my open window just right, creating the illusion of a sudden wind. When that happens, the freshness and the surprise settle upon my rest and I feel almost chilled.

And even though I'm generally up and ready for work before most of the birds have started calling and digging for breakfast, there's the occasional crow from a confused rooster or the distant chant of a bobwhite surging through the open window to remind me of the ruffled business of morning.

It's here, I find, in the breaking open of the calm night with the beginning sounds of a new day blaring through my open bedroom window, that I know the most and the best of happiness. It lasts only briefly, but it fills me up enough to last me the whole day. Morning is my easiest season and my own private party. I can't imagine waking to it in any other place.

Mama sleeps until the last minute, gets up when I'm ready to go, and rides with me to the Grill. She used to get dressed, go to the Grill, have breakfast, and go on to work at the funeral home. But that didn't last too many days. Being a late-morning person, she prefers to give herself a little more time to rouse. So now she just sits in the car while I get her a cup of Luther's coffee, which she takes back home while she starts over.

As far as I know, she hasn't talked to Liddy since the fight. She gets her hair done on Fridays, but usually it's after Liddy has already gone for the day. She doesn't talk to Tina about it, so I guess she doesn't hold the current state of affairs against her hairdresser. As far as her nails go, she tried to get me to do them one night, but I'm not too good with that little brush; so I think Aunt Doris did them the last time. She's been wearing a new shade called Pearl Ice that I'm sure Liddy wouldn't let be worn in public.

Liddy managed for the previous two Sundays to be gone from Grandma's house when we went over for the Ivy Sunday lunch. She's been off at the lake or out at a friend's; nobody's really pushed for information. So she and Mama haven't even run into each other over there, even though Mama's usually at Grandma's two or three times a week besides Sundays. It's been more than fourteen days now of pretending nothing's happened even though everybody knows about the fight. In the Ivy family, though, grudges are known to last a long time.

When Mama told me yesterday that she was going on the church retreat up in the mountains this weekend, I was surprised. Mama only dabbles in religion, having received her faith in small portions and over a period of years and in a number of places.

She goes Sunday mornings and Wednesday evenings to the Baptist church, to the fall tent revivals in McLeansville, and to the sunrise service every Easter. But she isn't one to travel with church folk. It's always seemed to me that she's soothed by the gospel but hampered by the attitudes of folks in the pews.

I figure her going has something to do with the piece I saw of the future about her and the preacher. Maybe something's starting to take hold of her. I watched them together on Sunday, and she seemed all nervous and jittery around him. When I asked her about it later, she just said his sermon had really touched her. But I knew that what took hold of her wasn't as uplifting or

as beneficial as the Holy Ghost. This was something else altogether, because unlike what happens to Rosa Hackett when she gets filled up,
Mama seemed rattled and sparse.

When I told Liddy yesterday afternoon that
Mama was going to be gone all weekend, thinking that she'd want to come over and stay with
me, eat popcorn, and watch a horror movie, all
she talked about was me going to Cordessa's
with her Friday night. I waved her off, but I figure she's going to bring it back up today.

It's Thursday, and Mama's already packed.
I'm sitting in the car waiting to take her for her
coffee, wondering if I should go in again and
make sure she's awake. Sometimes she drops
back off. But before I unbuckle my seatbelt and
open the car door, she's standing at the passenger side looking in the window.

"I wasn't sure you were up," I say as she gets
in the car.

She answers with an odd noise from the back
of her throat and whips down the visor to look
at herself in the mirror.

I pull out of the driveway slowly and without

turning on my lights. We've worked out a deal
with the people who live in the trailer below us.
If they'll be quiet when they get home from their
second-shift jobs at the battery factory, then
we'll be quiet and keep the lights low when we
leave for work in the mornings. So far, there
have been no problems.

"Luther got a bunch of late strawberries from
down over at the Sawyers' yesterday. He was
making pies when I left work. You want me to
buy us one?"

Mama snorts and makes a smacking sound
with her tongue. "I'm not gonna to be here, remember? But Grandma'd probably like one."

"When do y'all get back?" I ask, switching on
my driving lights as I turn onto the main road.
As usual, there's nobody else on the streets.

"Sunday afternoon. We're having church up
there." She slides way down in the seat, crosses
her arms, and closes her eyes. I recognize this as
a sign that she doesn't want to talk.

"What time are you leaving tomorrow?" I decide not to pay any attention to signs and signals.

"About two, I think." She doesn't move.

I want to ask her how she's getting to the church, since I don't usually get through with work until three-thirty on Fridays. But I know we can talk about it tonight before she leaves, so I let her doze.

The lights are on in a few houses, but most of the community looks like the sky—dark and quiet. It's a lonely stretch from the house to town, and I'm glad to have Mama's company even if she won't sit up and talk.

When I drive by the lake turnoff, I see a trailer sitting in the middle of the driveway. A tire is flat on the back right side and I notice a Nevada license plate. I guess they've been there a number of hours, because no flares are lit or flashlights burning, and I don't see anyone fixing the tire.

It's an old camping trailer, an Airstream, I think—the kind that looks like a giant silver bullet—and it's being pulled by a 1976 Chevrolet truck with a covered bed. Even in the dark I can tell about the makes and models of trucks because that was the one thing Daddy made sure me and Liddy got from him. That and a butterfly bush he planted behind the house.

I start to mention the trailer and the flat tire to Mama; but when I turn to look at her, I see a deer jump from the bank at the right side of the road. Since I think he's coming onto the road and across my path, I slam on the brakes and swerve to the left, crashing Mama onto the floor and my head into the steering wheel. When I look up—it must be some minutes later—Mama is pressed under the seat like a child, the deer has disappeared, and there's a red stream trickling down over my eyes.

"Good God, Tessa. Damn." She's still catching her breath. "What on earth just happened?" Mama tries to find her feet to support herself back into the seat but ends up using her knees and her elbows. Even so, she doesn't quite make it.

I have some difficulty answering. "A deer," I say, touching my forehead. As I gently explore the lump that's forming there, I start to feel sick.

Mama swishes and wiggles and finally unwedges herself from between the seat and the dashboard. She sits up next to me and turns my face to hers. "Jesus Christ, but that's going to be a goose egg." She brushes her hand across my hair and I wince and pull away.

"You seeing okay?" she asks. "How many fingers am I holding up? Are you dizzy or nauseated?"

I can't really say what I'm feeling. I'm all of a sudden tired and my head hurts. I'm still a little woozy, perhaps nauseated, and I think maybe I might have to throw up. I can't see her fingers because it's dark in the car, and I want to lay down.

Mama gets out and I can tell she's looking to see if we hit the deer. I want to know too, but I don't want to have to ask since my belly is starting to twist and my eyes throb. She comes over to my side of the car and opens the door. The light comes on suddenly—hurting my eyes.

She's rambling on, or so it seems. "Trauma . . . head injury . . . blackout." I don't know all that she's saying. It's like listening to her when she's down the hall and I'm in the kitchen. The words are muted and far apart.

I'm trying to adjust to the brightness of the light and the distorted sound of her voice when I notice a shadow behind her and hear the voice of a stranger.

"Y'all all right?" The voice is big and deep, strong like a tuba, but I can't see the face or the body that it comes from.

My head is now the bass line. Steady it throbs, in four-four time.

"She's hit her head," my mother says, her voice drifting away on the last word.

It feels as if I'm going underwater. I feel something wrapped around me come unsnapped as I start to fall off the boat maybe, or off the end of the pier; but then two big arms pull me back or under—I can't be sure which.

I hear him yell, "Sterling, unhook the trailer and bring the truck around."

Beat and *beat* and *beat*, it goes. The surface of the water and the voices above trail further and further away.

"No," someone says—my mother, I think. "Our car is all right. It's just a busted headlight. Put her in the back seat and I'll drive her to the hospital." I *think* this is her talking, and I *think* this is what she says.

And the big long arms that are connected to the broad-chested tuba man lift me up and lay me in the back seat. The water is deep; I land easy on the bottom. Tuba man swims or crawls in behind me after some discussion that I don't understand about who will drive and who knows how to get to the hospital and how I shouldn't fall asleep. Beside me, he feels firm and full.

My head—my spinning, tightened head—comes to rest on the giant tuba man's lap. He asks me all kinds of questions—what my name is, where I was going, did I hit the deer, and on and on and on. I'm not sure if I'm answering him or not. I hear the words sound out in my mind, but I can't feel my mouth and throat making noise. I think this must be how it is for Mama when she doesn't want to talk in the mornings.

My mouth is wet with the saliva that comes just before you throw up, sour and prophetic. I prepare myself for what's next. But just before I lift my beat-keeping, pounding, underwater head to vomit, the rear passenger door opens and a younger man leans inside. I can't see his face, but I know that he's the sun.

I turn towards the tuba man to ask him who it is and instead fill his lap with something that comes from way down deep inside me. Then I fall, face-first, headlong into it. And for a little while I leave my body, the tuba man, the back seat, and my mama's calls.

The hospital is a strange place to be if you're in a state of disorientation. Odd sounds surround you. Beeps and buzzes, hums and loudspeakers. Nothing seems stable, since you're either on a moving gurney or in a bed with wheels. You're stripped and showing while lots of people dressed in white stand around you, sticking things in your mouth, in your arms, in your ears, across your chest.

When I come to I'm confused about what I'm doing here, where I was going before I came, and even who I am. I think I'm awake, but I can't be sure. I see bursts of brilliant color and tiny focused lights, and I hear people talking around me, about me; but I'm a fog of fleeting images. The eyes of a bending frightened deer. The breaking of a dawn sky from down beneath the surface of water. The feel of a man's scratchy sweater. The sound of a woman hysterically singing. The smell of old dead fish. And the nearness of orange warmth, the color of tangerines and the coat of tigers, close and unprotected.

My eyelids are like caps on jars long ago stored and settled. I try to lift them by pulling them open with my brow, but my forehead is puckered and unmoving. It feels heavy on my skull. Voices and plastic tubing wrap around me, and I'm homesick for something I can't name.

I'm falling in and out of a dream. First there's a face right in front of mine, a stream of white piercing my eyes. Lips moving, but I can't understand the words. Question after question after question. I don't answer. Instead, I drop back and nestle next to the belly of a large, soft doe. She nudges me to lift up my head and look into the light, but I'm so sleepy and so comfortable that I don't want to move.

Then I lay upon her wide, smooth neck as she slowly rises to jump across the road by the lake, both of us staying long and easy in the air. The breeze of morning lifts us higher, and I close my eyes to lose myself in the sliver of sky that is ours.

Up above the tops of trees and across the fields of golden wheat, I rest upon the assurance that the doe is taking me to an easy place where I can sleep. A place warm and feathery, safe and quiet. A place far away from this chaos and distress. A place where my head won't be a drum. A place where I won't be pushed and pulled so violently by arms and worry and a roomful of strangers. A place where I can tilt into the sun.

I slope and slump and rest in the fur of the doe for I don't know how long, until finally I'm drawn back into the bright, noisy stiffness of a dimly green place that's all corners.

"Tessa, wake up. Tessa!"

It's a searing sound, a cry, a wail of danger. I feel the doe turn to it.

❧

"Tessa, *Tessa!*"

Over and over comes the cry. It won't stop, so I try to keep the doe from being distracted by it. She rises, though I try to pull her back down. I don't want her to leave.

"Tessa Lucille Ivy!"

"What?" I scream. "What?" I only want the voice to stop, the doe to come back, and my head to be still.

"It's important that you stay awake," the voice says. "Can you stay awake just a little while?"

I want to say no and go back to my dream; but the voice is so persistent, so familiar, so desperate for me to talk, that reluctantly I watch as the doe, who was my bed, jumps up and flies away. Finally, I turn towards the nagging sound.

I focus on my eyelids and try to pull them open. I use all of the energy that I have. I push and pull and wrinkle and loosen until at last I feel them unhinge and I blink.

It's Mama standing over me. I know her by the shape of her nose, the shifting of her eyes, and the tenderness of her touch. She smiles at me and slides the back of her fingers across my cheek. Tears pool and fall from her eyes. She reaches up to wipe them away, then places her wet hand back upon my face.

Liddy is there too. She has no makeup, looks plain like me, and bothered. She's holding Mama's other hand; and together like this, with Grandma and Aunt Doris close behind them, leaning around me, actually hovering over me, they become what I choose, the home I will have, and the dream that lets me rest.

"Hey, Baby Girl," Aunt Doris says, waving at me from behind Liddy's back.

"You scared us bad," Grandma says. She pats me on my leg. "*Real* bad. It was like you were straddling to the other side."

Just then a nurse walks in, pages the doctor on the phone by my bed to tell him that I'm awake, and suggests that my family leave the room while she checks my vital signs, adjusts my medications, and tests my vision and alertness. She tells them about the snackbar downstairs, says that it's open late, but I can see that they're not leaving.

"Late?" I ask. "What time is it?"

"Nine-thirty," my mother says.

"That's PM," my sister adds.

"Nine-thirty?" I repeat. "Nine-thirty? How long have I been in here? What happened?" Now I'm the one with the questions.

"We were driving to work and you swerved to miss a deer, smacked your head on the steering wheel when you hit the brakes." Mama runs her hands through her hair.

"I told you to trade in that old car for one with airbags," Doris says, clucking her tongue like an old hen. Mama turns to look at her sternly.

"Airbags probably wouldn't have really helped in this case, since you didn't run into anything," the nurse says.

She's short and bunched, has a cringing look about her. She reminds me of a missionary. Her face is pale white, like a sheet, and her hair is pulled tight in a bun. There's an air of haughtiness about her somehow. She sticks a thermometer in my ear and looks at the monitor above my head. She casts a light in my face and I blink.

Liddy rolls her eyes.

"Anyway," Mama continues, "you've been in and out of consciousness for almost two days now."

"Two days?" I say, surprised. "This isn't the same day?" I try to prop myself up on my elbows, but my arms feel loose like wings, and tubes tangle around me.

"Whoa there, young lady," Missionary Nurse says. She pulls my arms around to the front of my body and lays my head back on the pillow. "But Mamma, what about your retreat?" I ask. "Hush Tessa." Mama says reassuringly.

I hear a humming noise and feel the room start to turn and jerk like the first movement of a Ferris wheel. I sigh and close my eyes. Mama nudges the nurse away so that she can be back beside me. Just then the door opens again, and I strain once more to open my eyes.

"Well, look who's finally decided to wake up." It's Dr. Patterson. I assume he was somewhere in the hospital since he came so quickly. He's been the family doctor for as long as I can remember.

He's tall and old, with a tuft of gray hair, and he shuffles a bit now when he walks. He's kind and grandfatherly and never in a hurry.

"Hey, Mrs. Pinot, Bertie, Liddy." Always courteous, Dr. Patterson is known for his uncanny ability to remember names.

My family nods towards him in reply. Mama sticks out her hand and reaches for his, holding on like he's brought me back from the dead.

"We're so grateful for everything, Dr. Patterson." Mama is tearful again, and Grandma pats her on the arm.

"There, there, Bertie, everything's all right," says Dr. Patterson soothingly. "Our girl is just fine, aren't you, Tess?" Everyone moves away from the bed to make room for him.

I smile.

Missionary Nurse clears her throat—to push this reunion along, I presume. Dr. Patterson takes the hint; he points another light into my eyes, checks my chest and lungs, while Liddy and the nurse hold me up; and he has me follow his finger with my eyes. He asks me a few questions about my family, the president, and what I remember about the accident. Then he pulls a bandage off my forehead and gently touches the mound of flesh that's formed on my brow. It hurts beneath the pressure of his fingertips.

"That'll be sore for some time, I'm afraid." His breath smells clean, like mints. He pushes my hair behind my ear. "But you're going to be just like new." He sits down on the bed beside me and turns to my mother.

"We'll keep her through tomorrow morning just for observation, see if she can keep down some food, take a test, walk, that sort of thing; and if she does all right, I'll send her home over the weekend." He winks at me. "That okay with you, Number Two?"

That's what he calls me and Liddy sometimes, Number One and Number Two.

I manage another smile even though he's sitting against my leg and it hurts. "That's okay with me," I say.

"Y'all should go on home now that she's awake; it's late." He looks around at everybody.

They all nod towards him.

"Then I'll see you Ivy women in the morning," he says, taking the chart from the end of my bed and walking out with Missionary Nurse.

There's a sigh of relief from everybody in the room. I look into all of their faces, remembering who they are to me, remembering that they're extensions of myself—such a part of myself, in fact, that sometimes I can't recall which memories are mine and which are theirs. And seeing them now like this, gathered around me, I realize that all of who I am is a blending of these women, a blending of all the Ivy women from generations past.

They stand watching me for what seems like the longest time.

Finally Aunt Doris speaks. "Well, I think we need to go home and take a shower, get some sleep." She looks tired and washed-out.

"You okay by yourself here, Baby?"

I love it when Mama gets all sappy and sweet. Instantly I'm a child of four. I start to nod but decide against it as my stomach churns. "Yes, ma'am," I say.

Grandma rubs me on my leg and holds me at the ankle.

Liddy moves beside me and places her hand on top of mine, intertwining our fingers. "I'll see you in the morning, Skank," she says.

They stand that way for another few minutes, just staring at me as if trying to memorize my face. The attention grows uncomfortable after a little while and I yawn and look away.

Finally Liddy, Grandma, and Aunt Doris all sigh and walk out together, leaving Mama beside the bed. Grandma starts to turn in the wrong direction, but Doris nudges her the right way.

Mama fills me a glass of water and hands it to me. I hold the straw in my mouth and take a drink, but the water tastes so much like metal that I hand the cup back to her after only one sip. She sets it on my hospital table and slides the tray towards me so I'll be able to reach it when she's gone. Then I remember to ask, "Who were the two men who helped us after the accident?"

She's picked up her purse and is rummaging for her keys. "There weren't *two* men," she says. "Just one. Reverend Renfrow. He was in a trailer in the driveway to the lake. Do you want me to get you some juice before I go?"

I start to shake my head, then wince at the pain. "No," I say.

"He heard all the commotion and helped me get you here. But there weren't two—just him, Moses Renfrow, a black man traveling to the coast from somewhere out west."

She's found her keys; they jingle in her hand. "Moses," she says with a laugh. "Ain't that a great name for a preacher?"

"Nevada," I say. "His license plate was from Nevada."

Mama looks surprised that I would know this.

"Wasn't there somebody named Sterling?" I ask. "Didn't he call somebody to help us? Somebody who got in on the passenger side—his son or something?"

"No, Baby. I never met anybody named Sterling." She shuts her purse. Then she looks suspicious, like maybe I'm crazy. She glares at me and starts to ask me something else, but before she can we see Doris standing at the door.

"Come on, Bertie. Mama is getting frazzled."

"Yeah, okay, I'm coming." She looks over at her sister.

"Tessa saw somebody else get in the car when we came to the hospital."

"Well, you said there was some preacher." Doris isn't concerned. She tugs at the bottom of her jean shorts.

"No, somebody else." Mama and Doris hold a gaze.

"Oh," Doris says, all long and slow. "Somebody *else.*"

There's a long pause. Then Aunt Doris speaks. "Did he have a name?"

Mama answers for me. "Sterling," she says.

"Sterling?" Aunt Doris studies it. "Hmmm." She blows out a breath through her lips.

I hear Liddy and Grandma walk back through the door.

"What's the holdup?" Liddy asks. "We've held the elevator so long that the buzzer went off. Miss Nursey looks pissed." She raises her eyebrows and touches her fingers to her lips in a mocking sort of fashion.

"Tessa saw somebody else in the car when we came to the hospital. Somebody other than the preacher," Mama adds.

"Oh," Grandma says, just like Doris.

"So what?" Liddy asks for both of us.

"Yeah," I say, "what does that mean?"

The three of them fidget and look first towards and then away from each other.

Grandma moves over to stand by the bed. "Your great-grandmother Lodie used to see people before they really came too. It was a sign of trouble."

"Well, not always *trouble*," Mama adds worriedly. "Sometimes it was a good thing, like an angel."

Grandma shakes her head. "I think she just said that because she didn't want to worry us. I never remember nothing good coming from the folks she recognized. They were like forms of the devil that only she could see."

"She told me about Lester," Aunt Doris says. "He came to her in the likeness of a big black crow." She stops for a minute to think. "Was your premonition a bird or a four-legged creature?"

I think about the doe, but Mama answers for me. "It was a man."

Grandma and Doris suck in their breaths. "A man?" they ask in unison.

"So Tessa saw a man," Liddy exclaims angrily. "What's the big deal that Tessa saw a man?" She steps farther into the room and swings the door closed. "Maybe it was Jesus," she says, hushed-like.

Everybody sucks in their breath again. They all look at each other and shake their heads. They're a bundle of frayed nerves.

Finally it's Grandma who speaks. "The last time anybody in the family saw Jesus or a man who was said to be him appear out of nothing, the Ivy family lost everything."

"That's when they moved south and started over," Mama adds.

"That would have been your grandmother's mother, wouldn't it, Mama?" Aunt Doris looks over to Grandma as if to encourage her to tell the story.

Grandma nods. "Granny Ivy Littleton." She

shakes her head and sits down in the chair under the TV.

"She had just married Pete Littleton. He was from a nice family in Ohio, and the Ivys were living in nearby Pennsylvania. Granny was a teacher. She'd gone over to teach in the Littletons' hometown—Ashtabula, I believe. Anyway, they were young and fell in love, got married, and she got pregnant right away." Grandma takes off her glasses and rubs her eyes.

"So," she continues, "just hours before the baby was born, Jesus came to her. Now just hearing this story in a casual way, it might sound all comforting and sweet. But it wasn't that way. Jesus came in a fit of rage. All piss and vinegar, he was. And it scared her mightily." Grandma puts her glasses back on.

"Luckily, she remembered enough to tell her mama, who brought over the priest to bless the birth. But it was too late." Grandma stops and shakes her head as if she'd been there. "It was bad." She stops again.

Aunt Doris and Mama take each other by the hand. They know the story.

❧✲

"So," Liddy asks, "what happened?"

Grandma looks over to me as if maybe she shouldn't go on with the story.

"It's okay, Grandma; I want to hear." I turn gingerly on my side to look at her.

"Well, the baby was a girl."

"Lystra Ivy Littleton," Aunt Doris and Mama chime in together.

"Right," Grandma replies. "Lystra, named after Pete's mama. That's part of how you got your name, Liddy," she says, smiling over at my sister, who's studying Mama's chipped and splotchy fingernails.

"The labor was hard and long, but everything was fine. The baby was healthy and Granny survived the birthing. All went well for a couple of years. There was even another child."

"A girl," Mama says.

"Big Lucille," Aunt Doris adds.

Grandma reaches for my water glass and takes a sip.

"Then one day Lystra got real sick. Everybody just thought it was the cholera, but Granny Knew it was something more. She could tell by

84

the way the baby lay, all limp and useless, like a dishrag, and how she looked while she slept, like she was having a conversation or something." Grandma takes another sip of water.

"Granny was a religious woman so she prayed, remembering how Jesus had come to her right before the baby was born. She forgot, I guess, that Jesus was mad when he came and was all full of crazy rantings. She just remembered that he'd chosen her, come to her for something." Grandma lifts herself fully in the seat.

"Only this time Jesus didn't come." She pauses. A few seconds pass. "Lystra died."

Aunt Doris and Mama shake their heads.

"And then there was just this void, a hole, a rip that tore apart and emptied out her heart and yanked away her faith." Grandma grabs at the air like she's pulling at a weed. "And that's how it happened."

Liddy and I look at each other.

"*What* happened?" we say together.

"The downfall," Aunt Doris and Mama say in unison.

"The downfall," repeats Grandma.

There's a long, awkward silence while Grandma gets ready to tell the rest of the story. Liddy stops her before she can start. She's had enough of the family history lesson. "Look. Tessa has been in coma for a day and a half. She's just woke up!"

She puts her fists on her hips and looks disgusted. "I think maybe hearing a story about Jesus and the fall of the Ivy family may not be the best thing right now. Besides," she says, her voice rising, "I'm tired, and I want something to eat!"

Missionary Nurse suddenly barrels through the door, pushing Liddy aside. "This has got to stop!" she says, all strong and brassy, like church bells. "There are other patients on this unit who have to get their rest!"

She stops to recover her stern but quiet disposition, one hand on her heaving chest. "Now it's late, and I suggest you all go home and come back tomorrow. Visiting hours are over!" She ends her sentence with a giant snap of her tight-bunned head and then waits by the door until my family of women leave.

❦

Grandma gets out of the chair slowly. Aunt Doris holds her arm, and Mama walks out behind them like a child who's just been reprimanded by the principal. They all turn, one by one, and blow a kiss or give a wink.

Liddy, standing behind Missionary Nurse, shakes all over like she's having a fit and sticks her finger down her throat. I turn away because I don't want to laugh. It would make an angry woman angrier and would probably cause my head to hurt.

They all gather in the hall, Liddy joining them with a wave in my direction. Then Missionary Nurse turns the lights out and leaves, the door swiftly closing behind her. Grandma's words are left hanging in the air, and I'm suddenly alone in the darkness with a new fear of Jesus.

I close my eyes and try to push her story away, concentrating instead on the undone presence that spilled into our car yesterday morning. I remember being drawn to it, pulled into it like iron to a magnet; but whether it was good or evil, pleasant or mad, a premonition or real, I couldn't say.

It was—*he* was—the color of the inside lip of a marigold, bright and unspoiled. Peaked and sturdy. So orange that he was almost red. Deep and full and blooming. A fire that licked and blazed. I don't think I've ever witnessed such a brightness, except along the edge of my tea when I read the leaves a couple of weeks ago.

Thinking about it now, after hearing Grandma's story, I realize that I've never really imagined the color of Christ or how it would be to encounter him. Since I'm my mother's daughter and the kin of hedonistic men, I wouldn't claim to have much of a relationship with the Savior. I enjoy his stories, find the singing and talking in tongues at church entertaining, but I'd never call myself religious. I'm certainly not disciple material.

I've just never had a need for religion like some folks do. I'm comfortable with the notion that God and Jesus exist. I just don't need to get directions from them all the time. It seems to me we know all the important things anyway, like treating folks how we want to be treated, loving our enemies. This is commonsense stuff. I don't need to be dressed up, sitting in church all the time, to learn that. Besides, when I *am* in church the other women have a way, a smiling but unpleasant way, of making me feel sized up or discarded because of how I look or the trouble of my last name.

It isn't that I think I'm unworthy or inappropriate company for the Lord, like some people might consider. Truth be told, if I were questioned about the matter of who Jesus would choose to visit, I'd have to say that I think it makes perfect sense he'd want to spend time with the Ivys.

As odd as we might be—and that's a polite way of describing us—I still believe he'd have a lot more fun at one of our family Sunday dinners than he would at a church social or at Earlene Watson's house, the president of the Women's Circle.

She'd probably have him over for weak tea and those tiny cucumber sandwiches, all flat and white with only a hint of flavor. And she'd have him sitting in the living room on the sofa with the plastic wrap still on it, and she'd bore him to death with stories of her long-suffering life and complaints about the people who "take up so much of her time."

If he came to our house, we'd get out the best silverware and dishes, but it wouldn't be anything hoity-toity. Everybody would come as they are, and it would be an all-day Event. Uncle Ray would set out his cane-bottom chairs. Deedle would pull out his banjo and his mouth harp. Jasper would carry out his PA system he keeps locked in the box on his truck for karaoke shows. And in the kitchen, the pots on the stove would steam and whistle. The women would work together, sometimes fussing and sometimes humming, all of them making sure the plates were filled with just the right combination of goodness and texture.

We'd sing and tell dirty jokes and laugh about the dead ones; and we'd fill Jesus up with mudcake and lemonade spiced with Claudette's moon juice until he was so tired and so full and so worn thin from the grandness of it all that he'd fall asleep sitting straight up in a chair.

That's how it would be if Jesus came to an Ivy house for visiting, because that's how we do all our company.

But according to Mama and Doris and Grandma, Jesus doesn't come for socializing. They seem to think he comes only with judgment, an old sharp bone to pick, a pointed finger of damnation, since the last time he visited a family member he came in a fit of anger, when Lystra was born.

No wide blue eyes of comfort or handfuls of tender mercies, no broad shoulders to throw herself upon or ample, beating heart to silence approaching sorrow. To hear it from Grandma, Jesus didn't come for grace but rather came in a rage, as if the baby were a bad deed, a curse that he wanted stopped. And with that visit—and without the one she needed—he wreaked havoc on the mind and spirit of my great-great-great-grandmother, dampening the faith of generations.

And yet who's to say? Maybe my family got the story wrong. Not the action or the consequences but the way of telling it, the sorting it out and understanding it. Maybe Lystra was cursed and maybe Jesus knew it. Maybe just like Liddy Knows about love and Grandma Knows about storms, Jesus Knows too. And when he found out a baby was marked to die, he walked all the way from Paradise in a fit because he thought he could stop what was already on its way to happen. And when he couldn't or didn't, he ran away and hid. And that's why he didn't come when Granny Littleton kept calling for him. The burden of what he Knew but couldn't change was more than he could bear.

And then again, maybe the Ivy downfall didn't have anything to do with the coming or not coming of Jesus. Maybe it wasn't about a premonition or a sign. Maybe it had everything to do with the disappointment of having a sick and dying child. And maybe when that baby died, the death itself was what tore open Granny's heart, not some void or emptiness or reluctance on the part of Jesus to show up. Maybe it was just sorrow, just heavy, crushing sorrow. And because everybody knows that

❦

grief favors a villain, maybe Jesus was made to take the blame.

A beeping noise goes off near the left side of the bed. As I look over to see what's what, the lights are turned back on and Missionary Nurse comes into my room.

"It's the IV; you need a new bag." She reaches over and disconnects the alarm on the machine, then changes the bag that's hanging on a pole beside my head.

As she reaches over me I see a crucifix and a saint medal hanging around her neck, like the Catholics wear. I can't see what saint it is.

"You a Christian?" I ask.

"Sanctified, baptized, and redeemed," she replies, tugging at the old bag to disconnect it.

I watch her work, straining and yanking. She's as hard as dirt.

"And does Jesus ever come to you?" I move over in the bed so that I can see her face, which is all crossed in concentration and fatigue.

"Once," she says, dislodging the empty container and dropping it in the trash can triumphantly. Then she hangs the fresh one. It's full and distended like a new balloon. She checks the label, then turns the machine back on.

"He chased me like a tiger in the woods," she says, sliding her hands across the front of her starched white dress. "A big, lonesome tiger that knew my smell and my fear and my desire to get away; and I ran and hid and ran some more, but he was always there, hungry and ravenous for my sinful soul."

She adjusts the pillow behind my head without the slightest consideration that it might hurt. "But finally I turned from my running and my erroneous ways and lay myself down before him."

"Did he pounce you?" I ask.

"No," she says, writing something on my chart. "He lifted me upon his back and rode me home."

I think about the doe from my dream and smile.

Then she pulls out some graham crackers from the pocket in her dress and places them on my table. And she holds out a cup of cranberry juice, turning the straw towards me so that I can drink it from her hand. It's sugary and comforting, and I consider the possibility that maybe Missionary Nurse isn't as far away from the Kingdom of God as I had thought.

3

The Cut of
Mr. Jenkins's Eye

❧ I know that I'm not at home because the first sound I hear isn't that of a deep-throat grass frog or a black cricket singing. It's not the protective call of the male cardinal or the drone of an early katydid. It's the rumbling of the meal cart going down the hall. And like the whoosh of a plane landing next door, the sound drowns out everything else.

I also know that I'm not at home because, unlike the moist and fragrant heat that fills our house, the air in this room is as chilled as the blast of air that escapes from the meat locker when I open the door at Luther's. The thin blanket and the raggedy, open-backed gown I'm wearing offer little warmth. It's cold and loud here; and I long to be in my own bed, with sheets that don't make noise when I move and a window that opens into our backyard garden.

Someone comes in and drops a tray on my bedside table without a word, probably thinking I'm still asleep. I don't remember the last meal I had, but the gurgle in my gut suggests that it might have been awhile. Even in the tight band of this morning's disorientation I'm alert enough to consider that maybe I could eat a little something. I realize, however, that eating would require me to change positions; and it's taken me a very long time to settle myself in such a way that I'm not cold. So now I have to decide which is more important, to eat or to stay warm. Since I figure that a nurse will be in momentarily to take my blood or its pressure, I decide to relinquish the posture of comfort and take the offered nourishment.

"Hey, you up?" It's Liddy, and she charges in my room, turning on the lights and pushing aside furniture. Now I know I'll have to move.

When I'm clear enough to open my eyes, I see

that she has her hair in a ponytail, pulled through the back of the knock-off Tommy Hilfiger hat she got from a man in the parking lot at the mall. She looks slim and tan and perfectly dressed for summer. Everything matches, blue and white, crisp and clean, all the way down to her new shiny Keds.

When I see her like this, all made up and cute, it makes me think that maybe Liddy and me aren't so bad-looking. Even though she fancies fashion a little more than I do, wears makeup, and gets her hair cut and styled, she's still my mirror; and this morning, with half-opened eyes, I like what I see.

I blink and yawn. And now that I start to wake and rise, I notice things, like that my teeth are coated in medicine and last night's snack. And my arm hurts from the needle lodged inside my vein. My head feels heavy and tethered, and I can feel that my hair is matted and sticking out.

"Ol' Doc says he'll let you go home today if you can eat breakfast, pee, and walk down the hall." She stands at the side of my bed. "We just saw him at the front door." When I don't respond immediately, she shakes me a little to make sure I'm up.

I open my eyes again and press the button to raise the head of the bed. My breakfast sits in front of me. I lift off the top and Liddy leans forward to see what's on the tray.

"Mmmm," she says, taking the towels off the chair and sitting down. "Pot liquor and Jell-O, along with coffee and grape juice; that'll be tasty." She unfolds a towel and drapes it over her legs, tucking it under on each side. "Why they keep it so cold in here?"

"I don't know," I say. "Where's Mama?" I brush down my hair with my hands, remembering as I touch it the lump in my brow. I sit up slowly, pulling the sheet and blanket around me. Then I unwrap the napkin and the silverware, take the lid off the broth, and stir sugar in my coffee.

"She stopped by the phone to call Lynch. Somebody's dying on the third floor." Liddy pulls a nail file from her pocket and begins to file the nails on her left hand.

"She got all tense and batty this morning, couldn't say who it was; then when she got here she finally figured it out." She dusts off her fingers.

"Anybody we know?" The broth is too hot; it burns my tongue.

"A Mr. Whitehead or Whiteface or White-something. I've never heard of him. Had a big policy though, I think. Mama seemed excited." She sticks the file back in her pocket and holds her hands together, out in front of her.

"You still staying at Grandma's?" I take a spoonful of Jell-O. It's red and very firm.

"Nah. She snores too loud, and I swear she talks to herself. I went home the night you hit your head."

"Hmmm," I say in response.

"Things are fine." She says it like I don't believe her.

"I apologized to Mama for jumping her, and she apologized for bruising my lip." Liddy touches her mouth to feel if there's a scar; then she pulls her ponytail tighter.

"What about Cordessa's?" I put down the

spoon, feeling worn out after just a couple of bites.

"Oh, I'm still working at Cordessa's. That didn't change. In fact, I've got to go in at five tonight. It's been really busy."

I take a sip of coffee as a morning nurse I haven't seen before comes in and checks the hardware around my bed. She says somebody will be back when I've finished breakfast. Then she looks from me to Liddy like she's seeing double, which she is. "Twins," she says, like we don't know it.

Liddy gives her that "You're an idiot" look to discourage any further comment. The nurse lifts her eyebrows, purses her lips, and goes out the door.

"What did Mama say about that—about you still working at Cordessa's?" I slide down in the bed to rest.

"She hasn't said anything about it." Liddy straightens her hat. "Except she said that I'd have to get a ride because she doesn't want to be at home with you tonight and not have no car."

"What happened to the truck?" Liddy has been

driving Daddy's old truck that he didn't take with him when he left since she was fifteen.

"It's got a busted belt. Deedle went to pick one up for me, but they said it would be next week before one came in." She looks bored.

"And how are things at Tina's House of Style?" I ask, trying to pick up her interest and find out what I've missed.

"Same as usual. Luther needs you at the Grill, though. He tried to get me to fill in for you." She smiles at me. "I told him I wasn't the morning type."

"That's for sure!" I agree. "What's more is that you ain't the serving type."

She kicks the bed a bit. "I serve! I do manicures, remember? How do you think I'm able to do all those country club women's nails?"

"Because you know you can laugh at them when they leave and because you know that somewhere there's a tip involved." I fluff up my pillow with the arm that doesn't have the IV in it.

"Like you don't waitress because there's tips?" she asks, sounding like she knows she's right.

❋

"No," I reply, "I do my job because I enjoy watching people eat."

Liddy snorts like she knows I'm lying, and I laugh at the thought that I could be so high-minded.

We're some pair, Liddy and me. Neither one of us is real selfless or sensitive. Sometimes people mistake us for being shallow, but it's not that; we're just uncomplicated. We know what we like, and we aren't afraid to go after it. And for the most part, we're pure. We don't get distracted or divided about stuff.

We're like all the Ivy women—thick-lipped, headstrong, and sturdy. We've got good souls and are easy with our welcome. None of us is proud or stuck up. And we're as loyal as they come. Any one of us, without a thought, would take down anybody who threatened an Ivy.

"Well, well, looks like you're feeling a lot better this morning. What's for breakfast?" Mama swings in the room looking all refreshed and glowing.

"Meat runoff and grape juice," I answer, sitting back up to eat some more.

❧

Liddy pulls her legs up in the chair so Mama can walk around to the bed. "You get hold of Lynch?"

"Yes." She moves over to the side of the bed. "He wasn't real happy." Mama looks at my food and draws up her nose. "He had to cancel his golf game tomorrow and call in Billy Maiden from Fayetteville. He'd gone for the weekend to visit his wife's family."

"Has the man died yet?" I ask.

"Oh, goodness no. He's got at least a day or so to go." She puts down her purse and lifts up the cup of broth to smell it. "Chicken or beef?"

I shrug my shoulders.

She sets the cup back on the table and starts arranging things on my tray. Puts the coffee on the back part, shakes and opens up the juice, searches for a straw and sticks it in the container. She finds another spoon in the table drawer and puts it in the soup, moving the one I've already used near the Jell-O.

"Did you sleep okay?" she asks, examining her work.

I nod.

❧

"Old Lady Nurse from Hell didn't call for more blood or tape your mouth shut?" Liddy moves around in the chair so she can see me better.

"No," I reply, blowing on the broth. Mama takes it from my hands and cools it for me.

"You know, she really wasn't so bad," I say, picking up the Jell-O spoon. "She gave me her own snack." I point with my chin at the foil from the graham crackers.

"Not so bad?" Liddy asks, all self-righteous and surprised. "She almost called security on us! She practically followed us down the elevator!"

"She was a little on the tightly strung side," Mama agrees, winking at me.

"Tightly strung? Try stretched and over the edge. She was a bitch!" Liddy crosses her arms over her chest.

Mama puts down the cup and rolls her eyes. "Oh, she probably has to be that way to get her job done. I'm sure it can be downright dangerous in here with people all doped up and flailing about." She takes the clean spoon and stirs the soup.

"Yeah, like Tessa the first night when she almost took out that orderly who came to rebandage her head."

I look over to Liddy, puzzled. I don't remember this.

"Oh, by the way," Mama says to me, waving off Liddy's last comment, "did your sister tell you?" She bends down to pick up a napkin that's fallen. "There *was* another man."

I'm confused, still trying to recall the orderly I must have decked.

"In the car," she continues. "Remember?"

"Doris and Grandma thought it was Jesus," Liddy adds, circling her finger about her head to indicate that they were crazy.

"With Reverend Renfrow?" Mama reminds me. "His son, I guess." Mama takes the Jell-O from me and waits to hear something that shows I understand what she's talking about. "Sterling?" she prompts.

I crane my head towards her and put down the spoon. "There *is* a guy named Sterling?"

"Yeah, I don't know how I forgot about him. He came to the car when we were about to leave." She hands me the broth, apparently convinced that I haven't eaten enough. "I thought more about it when I got home last night and you were right. I guess in all the muddle I just forgot."

Mama motions for Liddy to get up and give her the seat.

Liddy pulls her legs down slowly and reluctantly moves to the window. She leans against the sill with her feet propped on the radiator.

"Anyway, there was a boy named Sterling," Mama says, easing down into the chair. "He didn't come with us, and Reverend Renfrow never mentioned him in the car. But I guess he drove on after we got here and picked the old man up. Once they got you in the emergency room and I was able to go back with you, I never saw the Reverend again." She crosses her legs at the ankles and sighs.

"When we went by the lake drive the next morning, the camper was gone," Mama adds. "I didn't even get to thank him." She refolds the towel Liddy used and places it on the floor by the bed.

"So your Jesus was really a young black boy who drives around with a man named Moses." Liddy smiles as she plays with the blinds on the window.

When she turns the slats as open as they'll go, I see the spill and pull of the morning sun, its rays a vivid orange-yellow. Then she pulls the slats up and I'm drawn to the sun and blinded by it, paralyzed in it. The color blasts straight through a fog and aims dead-center for my head, rousing some old dream. I'm in no mood to dwell upon it, so I turn my face back towards the food and my mother's words.

"How you could remember him, I don't know. He was there only for a second." She jumps up to help me because I almost drop the coffee cup.

"He just opened the door and looked in. I don't think he even said anything, did he?" She holds the cup for me while I take the straw from the juice and put it in the coffee. After I take a drink she puts it down.

"No," I say and turn to Liddy, who's shadowed in the light but who, I can tell, has a curious look, as if maybe she's thought of something new.

We're all distracted then by the nurse, who clears away my breakfast things, takes out the IV needle, and gives me a sponge bath. She's gentle and not very talkative, a dark-skinned woman who's exact and formal. Liddy brushes my hair and takes the rubber band from her own ponytail to tie mine up. I wash my face myself—except for my forehead, which still has a bandage on it—and change my underwear. Mama rubs some lotion on my back and gives me a T-shirt and sweat pants to put on and I feel like I have just walked out of a grave.

After I rest a little while, I have a examination from Dr. Patterson—things that includes things like reciting the ABCs and counting numbers backwards. He seems pleased that I can recall so much and says he'll do the discharge paperwork while I have a stroll. When I get back, I'll be able to go home.

Mama gets me up to take the required walk. She's brought her bedroom shoes from home and slides them on my feet. Then I stand and move to the door. I feel wobbly and spent, so Mama walks on one side and Liddy on the other. Together we go out into the hall and down to the other side of the unit.

It's odd to me how quick your legs can forget what they're supposed to do. It seems almost like I have to tell them, "Move straight out in front, now bear the weight, now the other, come on, quicker, left then right." How could I have lost such a basic thing as walking in only two days? A muscle starts to twitch on my right side. I stop a minute.

"You sick?" It's Mama. She's holding me up higher than Liddy, so I'm lopsided in addition to feeling weak.

I shake my head. "Just need to rest."

We've gone about thirty feet, out of the unit and into the hallway.

"You want me to get a wheelchair?" she asks.

I see her face all tangled in worry, hoping I'm not going to collapse.

"No," I say, doing my best to give her a reassuring look.

Just then several hospital workers—nurses

and doctors and technicians—run past us to a room on the other side of my unit. We stand up against the wall to get out of their way. Carts and machines, men and women frantically hurry past. They're like clowns getting in the little Volkswagen at the circus. How they'll all fit in there, I don't know. Finally, after the last one manages to get in, they close the door. But we can still hear them in there, throwing things and yelling about the passage of time. We just can't *see* the trauma.

I look at Mama to see if she Knows what's going to happen, whether it's someone other than Mr. Whitehead whose time has come. She just shakes her head no and closes her eyes—to pray, I suppose.

"You're not going to barf, are you?" Liddy has only just realized that we've stopped for a bit. She asks not because she's concerned about my health but because she's worried that something might mess up her new pair of white sneakers. She bends down and wipes them off, looking at them from several angles to make sure they haven't gotten scuffed or dirty. Even the soles are clean.

"If I do, I'll turn the other way," I tease.

"Yeah, like you turned the other way on that preacher." She stands up and leans into me, readjusting her shoulder under my weight and picking me off my feet in the process. "That man is probably still trying to clean out his britches."

When I think about that poor old preacher man and how I vomited in his lap, I start to get tickled. It's a funny image; and even Mama, when she begins to remember, starts to laugh.

"Kind old man, couldn't say a thing." She's talking in spurts now, phrases coming out around the laughter.

She shakes her head. "And I couldn't get you up and drive at the same time. It was unbelievable!" She's bent halfway over by now.

"You lying face down in his lap, passed out in your puke, and him trying to get out of the way without hurting you. It was like something from that *Funniest Video Show* thing on TV!"

I'm laughing too, the thought of some strange

man holding not just my head but also the insides of my stomach seeming funnier and funnier.

Not far from the room of the patient in distress—the patient all the hospital staff have crammed in to save—the three of us are out of control. We're slapping our legs, slapping each other's legs, almost falling over laughing. Mama's talking about how the car still stinks. Liddy's making puking sounds while I'm trying not to slide down to the floor. We're a sideshow, a noisy, disruptive comedy act; and I think how lucky we are that the patient's door and the doors to the unit have been closed. I'd hate for anyone to think we're laughing at the arrival of someone's gravest hour.

Just then, as I'm trying to straighten myself up and catch my breath, the elevator door right behind us opens and three men in suits walk out.

Since we're right in their way, Mama pulls me to the side, keeping her arm under mine; while Liddy, unaware of what's happened, stays in the middle of the hall. As they step out, first one and then the others, I see that the second man is Mr.

Tyrus Jenkins. He looks right in our direction but doesn't even notice us.

I don't know if I've ever been this close to him or seen Mama near him before, since we live on different sides of town and all. But it seems like she freezes up when he goes by; she gets all stiff and prickly, like a briar. Her grip on my arm tightens and I almost feel bruised. Liddy doesn't see and doesn't care. She's still acting like she's sick, making those heaving noises, though she's laughing by herself now.

One of the other two—the youngest one, the last one, the one who looks the most out of place in a suit and in the company of Mr. Jenkins— stares at Liddy like he's wondering whether he should call somebody; he clearly thinks she's really sick.

I assume he's a son—he's got that look about him—but I've never met him. The Jenkins children never associated with the rest of the community; they always went to the private school between here and Goldston. He doesn't appear to be much older than me and Liddy, which fits with what I know of the family. He's tall and handsome and careful, but when Mr. Jenkins hands him a disapproving glance, he changes his focus and turns away.

The three men step around us or through us, like we're pieces of furniture or boxes or an obstacle in their pathway. I strain to see the look in Mr. Jenkins's eye, reminded of the leaf in my tea, but he walks by too quickly. As I'm left in his wake, I'm struck by a strange wind, almost a howling, that seems to follow them.

When I turn back to Mama, I see that her face has gone pale. She looks blank, pinched, and lost. She's the same shape, the same woman, but with the air pulled out. I touch Liddy on the shoulder and she stops joking and looks at Mama, then at the backs of the three men moving silently down the hall.

"What is it, Mama?" I ask. The elevator door closes behind us with a click, startling her. "Is it Mr. Whitehead? Is it his time?" I ask. "Is it the code-blue?"

I'm never sure what it's like for Mama when she starts to Know. Sometimes it happens so fast that I hardly observe anything out of the ordinary. I just see her close her eyes and listen real still, her fingers to her chest, and then hear her make the phone calls. But sometimes the Knowing seems to make her sick or washed-out, like she's had a seizure; and she'll stay that way for a few minutes, then get up and go to bed. But we've never discussed what the gift does to her, so I'm not clear about the physical results of her paranormal displays.

She just shakes her head, like she's moving back, touches up her hair, and reaches under my arm. "We need to get you back to your room," she says.

Liddy and I bear traces of the same confusion. Neither of us dares to voice our questions out loud, though, so we get back in position and slowly walk to my room.

When we finally get back, I'm exhausted. Someone has stripped my bed and put my things in a bag down at its foot. I'm so tired that even though there are no sheets, I lay down anyway. Mama gets me a drink of water.

Not long afterwards a new nurse hurries in. She's young, wide, and flustered, her face splotched and red. She flits around like a mayfly, pulling down and closing the blinds that Liddy had opened wide and to the top. Then she pushes aside the IV pump and turns off the monitor. She says that I can go home but should wait for the wheelchair and the volunteer who will escort me.

She explains precautions and directions for my discharge to Mama while she pulls out the lining in the trash can and slides the bed against the wall. She turns on the water, washes her hands, jerks out and uses a paper towel, and throws the crumpled paper in the trash-can liner that she's dropped at her feet.

"A new patient is coming in," she says, pulling the dirty linen into a bundle at her chest. "Another head injury." She looks at herself in the mirror. "Any questions?" Her hair is a crown of wet, sweaty curls. She looks as if she's worked all night, but I haven't seen her until now.

Mama is still reading the discharge papers, still trying to take in all that the nurse has said. Liddy is standing at the door, ready to go, so I just smile and wait for Mama to answer. But before anyone can say a thing, the nurse scurries past the three of us and I hear her holler that somebody needs to mop the floor in my room.

I close my eyes, but it isn't long before an old man with an ill-fitting red jacket adorned with a nametag that reads SULLIVAN comes into the room pushing a chair. He's whistling some showtune that I can't quite recognize.

"Ah, the queen's ride," he says, all cheery. He's lively and obviously pleased with the day.

I wait a minute, hoping for a burst of energy, then get off the bed and sit down in the wheelchair. Mama stands and announces that she'll go on ahead to pull the car up to the door. She stuffs the papers in her purse and takes my bag of things.

"You girls didn't get in any fight now, did you?" Sullivan asks, grinning as he looks at the bandage on my head. His teeth are square and white.

"No, sir," I say, thinking what a friendly and pleasant man he is.

Liddy waits while he adjusts the chair to fit

my feet. I think that maybe I should help; but I feel a bit funny when I look down, so I just try to keep my legs out of his way. He's whistling again—this time "Swing Low, Sweet Chariot." When he finally gets the plates adjusted, he pulls himself up by the handles and pushes me out of the room, saying, "And ladies, away we go!"

Sullivan is tall and brown as cinnamon with a mouth that takes up his whole face. He's skinny and raw-boned, but his arms are strong and he's quicker with his hands than his age would suggest. His eyes are milky, clouded over like a blind man's; but he seems to see quite well. He has a long gait and a clear, deep voice.

As we head out, he talks to everybody we go by. "Hey, Girl!" "Where you been, Sweetheart?" "How come I ain't got no sugar from you?"

And all the women he speaks to bask in his attention, touching him on the arm, darting their eyes around him with a blush, or throwing both hands towards him while turning their heads like he's telling some wonderfully luscious lie.

Liddy is walking beside me. "What was that

all about, out there in the hall?" She doesn't notice Sullivan's flirting.

I remember that Mama still looked a little gray when she left, and I say, "I don't know."

"You darlings parked in the circle or on the deck?" Sullivan asks as he wheels me out of the unit and towards the elevator.

"Deck," Liddy replies.

"Wasn't that Mr. Jenkins in that group?" she asks me.

"Yeah," I say, looking up at her. "Why you reckon she got so spooked?"

Before she can answer I call out a good-bye to the nurses at the station, who yell back, wishing me good luck. The young wide one who flits is nowhere to be found. We go through the double doors to the unit.

"Mr. Tyrus Jenkins!" Sullivan says, pulling out all the syllables to make it last a long time. He almost sings it.

We stand at the elevator until it opens and we go in. "Can you push number one?" he asks Liddy as we step inside.

She pushes the button and the door closes. I

feel a bit uncomfortable that Sullivan has been listening to our conversation, so I sit quietly.

"Ah, but there ain't nothing like the fixed eye of Satan on a young woman." The comment seems harsh and out of character, and I'm not sure who Sullivan is talking about.

Liddy brushes her arm across my shoulder and Sullivan starts to whistle again.

We stop on the first floor and the door opens. The elevator is right behind the information desk, close to the main door. Looking through it, I can see Mama in the car at the end of the covered walkway. Liddy holds the elevator door while Sullivan tilts the chair to get it over the cracks. We move past the desk and towards the front door.

When the hospital door opens automatically, a sweltering wall slams into us, forcing my eyes shut. I've forgotten the lowness of summer, the drag of the thick, listless sky. But still, even in the surprise of the late-morning's intensity, I'm glad to be out of the air-conditioning. My chest swells with new air. The sun is bright and high and burning. I squint to see Mama.

❧

"Oh Lord, yes," Sullivan says, like he prefers the outside too. He leads me down the covered walkway to the car, humming something low and sad. He sounds like the inside of church.

He pushes the chair sort of fast so that there's a breeze stirred up around me, and it makes me laugh out loud. Then he puts on the brakes real quick-like just as we get to the curb, causing me to squeal.

I pull my feet out of the props as he walks around, still smiling at the sudden joy the ride brought me. He bends down in front of me and whispers, "You don't have to see everything to know." Then he winks and stands up again. He opens the car door while I get in, shuts it behind me, and stays at the curb, whistling.

Liddy goes around and gets in the front passenger seat. I lean in so that I can see Mama in the rearview mirror. Her color is back.

"Well, that was quick," she says. "Who'd you have pushing you?"

"Sullivan," I say, turning to see him. He grins and nods in our direction.

Mama nods back at him. "He looks like the cat

that ate the canary. What was he saying?"

Liddy shifts towards me, unsure what he'd meant about Satan.

"Something about evil," she says, sliding herself back around in the seat to face the front.

"And the way we see it," I add, straining to find his face in the sun.

Mama makes a funny noise, like a laugh or a sigh, rolls down the window, sticks her arm out, puts the car in gear, and drives away.

The old cinnamon man who sang me out of the hospital, the long cut of a familiar eye, and the surfacing of latent trouble melt and blur in the summer heat. I realize, however, that I won't soon forget what has just passed.

4

The Rising of the Sterling Sun

❀ Mama and Liddy seem to pay a lot more attention to me now that I've had a head injury. They seem downright jittery since I've been back home.

"Can I get you some more soda?" Mama will ask when I'm just laying on the couch watching *Andy Griffith* reruns.

"You want me to paint your nails?" Liddy will offer when she gets off work in the evening.

I'm surprised by the concern and the close eye of these women I used to think were never rattled. Cautious and watchful of me, they treat me like I could fall over any second. I've been back four days, but they make it seem like I'm only minutes away from some critical surgery.

Doc Patterson says I shouldn't go to work for a week, so I'm taking it pretty easy. Not since I had my tonsils out in fourth grade have I had such care and time to think.

Mama stayed home with me the first couple of days, but with the Whitehead funeral and all she had to get back to work. Liddy goes in around ten every morning. And since Aunt Doris works first shift at the tire factory, Grandma Pinot is the only one I see before supper.

She stops by and brings me lunch, washes my hair, or changes my sheets, rolling them back in an invitation for a nap. She and I play cards and watch the soap operas, which she calls "her stories." And I've helped her string the early half-runners that Deedle grows in the garden behind her house. She's helped the days pass swiftly.

She won't be coming over today, though, because Jasper is taking her to the farmers' market in Raleigh. She likes to go during tobacco harvesting, just to hear the auctioneers. Grand-daddy Jacob used to call prices, and she finds it comforting to go back every year and sit in the company of her husband's only true love.

It's early for tobacco, but somebody told Jasper they were looking over stored plants from last year. Grandma jumped at the chance to experience the sale so soon in the season. She says the smells of the aged yellow leaves and the rhythm of the calling and the clicking of old men's wooden canes on the cement floor bind her up in a way nothing has since Granddaddy Jacob died.

Her marriage is the only one in the family that I know of to have survived the recklessness and the troubles inherent in the Ivy clan. Not that Granddaddy Jacob was any saint. He could be downright ornery, in a nasty way that made Mama and Doris scared of him. But to me and Liddy he was as thrilling as licorice-flavored shaved ice.

I still remember how he'd stand on the porch and call us. Since that was before two rows of trailers lay between the houses, we could look through the window and see when he was home. He'd step outside and holler out our names and we'd quit whatever we were doing and race to the house. We realized that if he was calling, he either had a great story to tell or had picked us up something from the auction. Either way, we knew we were in for a treat.

He'd bring us caramels or little porcelain toys or strands of glass beads. Or he'd sit us up on the railing and tell us about the smallest horse in the world—one that you could hold in the palm of your hand—or the alligator that ate her own children. He was the moon to us when we were small, big and soothing and full. We didn't hear the stories of his drinking or his heavy hand until the ground over his casket was grassy and flat. Grandma saw no need to spoil our ideas of a good man.

When I asked her one time a year or so ago how she knew she was in love, how *anybody* knows, she reached out and drew her fingers from the top of my head down, closing my eyes and continuing along my face until she brought her fingers and thumb together, gently pulling my lips into the ends of her touch.

"It's like melting," she said. "Everything you

thought was important just dissolves into the taste of some wretched man's kiss."

I remember opening my eyes, surprised to hear her talk that way.

"Once that happens," she added, "nobody can tell you a thing."

I've never kissed a man, unless you count family. And that's just for greetings and good-byes—kisses on the cheek, usually. Daddy loved to kiss us when we were small, but he always did it just to make us laugh. Deedle isn't much for affection, and Granddaddy's been dead so long I can't remember what he did. Uncle Ray seems frightened of girls, big and small, so he's never put his face near mine. So even with menfolk who have a common bloodline, I haven't learned exactly how to twist my head or what to do with my teeth.

Liddy tried to teach me one time how to french, but the thought of my sister's tongue in my mouth was too gross even for us. So she just had me practice on the mirror.

Even without the experience, though, I think I'll be a good kisser if I ever get the chance. I've got good lips, broad and soft. I learn things real quick and I'm open to trying new stuff. Fresh breath is real important to me and I haven't ruined myself with smoking or too much dental work. I wouldn't consider myself messy or too rigid. I think I'm just right, somewhere in the middle between relaxed and attentive. But it sometimes seems to me that I won't ever get the chance to try it out and see.

Liddy says I should get out more, go to more dances, hang out with other people our age. But I don't know—I'm just not as comfortable in big groups as Liddy is. Besides, I know all these boys, and none of them strikes me as very good at anything tender or slow like kissing. I figure if I'm meant to exercise my lips and learn the temptations of the flesh, it will—*he* will—come to me.

Today being Wednesday, I remember that Mama will stay at work a little later and stop by the church on the way home. Most Wednesdays I get a ride home with Shirley after work at the Grill, since she lives in the park, or I walk down to Tina's and wait for Liddy. But today, since I'm already at home, I don't have to think about it.

Liddy's going to Cordessa's right at five. They're having a meeting about what to do for the upcoming July Fourth party. Mama will be gone until after eight, since she stays for choir practice too. So I'll be at home for a longer day today by myself; and I'm thinking about watching an old movie, reading the stacks of magazines Mama's brought from the funeral home, or maybe even taking a walk, though Grandma said a storm would roll through late in the evening.

I like to go back behind the house, past the garden and through the old wooden fence my great-grandfather put up years ago when we had cattle. There's a long trail through rows of pines, across a meadow, and past the road that goes to Sandy Creek.

If it's not been raining in awhile, the creek bed is dry and you can take a shortcut that leads right around to the lake. Not many people know about the trail because it's real grown up on the other end, the one near the lake; and most folks don't gad about our place where the trail is more clearly marked. So the path feels unspoiled and adventurous; and I'm never anxious about coming up on anybody. I just feel a little worried sometimes about the snakes.

When I was eight, I got bit by baby water snakes. I was barefooted down at the creek, hunting for arrowheads and polished rocks, when I stuck my toes into a bed of young moccasins. The tiny brown cords draped across my ankle and slid along like ribbons of poison. I yanked my foot away right quick, but I was bitten three times across the top and once on the bottom of my heel. It swelled quickly, so it's a good thing Deedle was close by hunting. He tied a handkerchief around my calf and carried me to the hospital. They drained the venom and bandaged my leg, but they couldn't do anything about my nightmares of being pulled down into the muddy water by strings of snakes.

Since then, I never go barefooted outside; and I hardly ever go back to the mouth of Sandy Creek, unless I know that snake season is long since past. Liddy says I need to get over it, but I don't see how she could possibly understand the horror of landing in a nest of hungry baby reptiles.

The freshness of this memory almost keeps me from going outside, but the day is breezy and fairly cool for late June. I hear the birds through the open windows, the tractor from the farm nearby; and now that I've had my lunch and feel nourished, I suddenly have the urge to step beyond the mowed area of our yard and walk down to Crystal Lake.

I wear long pants and an old shirt, two pairs of socks, and the thick, rugged hiking boots that I bought last winter. I clip up my hair, throw on sunglasses, and lather my arms and neck with insect repellent. I grab a stick, fill a bottle with water, wrap up a few cookies, and holler for our old dog, Burlap, who comes out from under the house, surprised to see me out. Brown and woolly like an old sack of flour, he bounces ahead, then turns to make sure I'm still following.

I walk through the garden first, since I'm the only one who really pays it any attention. Grandma and Aunt Doris have their own, and

Liddy and Mama couldn't care less about what I put out every year. Weeds have sprung up between the plants and threaten to take over if I don't get back and hoe pretty soon. I tighten the twine on some of the tomato plants that have started to droop, and I make a mental note to cover the peppers with Sevin Dust since worms have started eating large holes in the leaves. I straighten out some of the cucumber vines that have drifted over into the watermelon patch and check the size of the cantaloupes, which still look like tiny balls of fur.

The second planting of radishes need to be thinned out; and the squash are filled with fat humming bees dancing from one end of the garden to the other. I stand back and smile at the lushness of the early growth, the tender sprouts spreading, stretching, becoming stronger and stronger, the produce forming from seed to flower to food. I love summer mostly because of what happens in this small patch of ground just at the edge of where I sleep. The plants are alive and in deep conversation with the sun and the evening showers and the bearers of pollen that help them grow.

I've loved putting my fingers in dirt for as long as I can remember. And I've saved and counted seeds, cared for and nurtured feeble green life, so that I'm responsible for just about every bit of plant life around this house and yard. Though I laugh and love at many places close by, I'm happiest lifting food and beauty and remedy from the cold, dark brownness of the earth.

Burlap stops at the edge of the yard and lays down, teased, since he thinks I am only staying here, at the garden. So that when I wash off my hands at the water spigot and pick up my stick and walk past him, he doesn't even get up. It isn't until I put one leg over the lowest rung in the fence and touch down on the other side that he jumps up and barks and runs ahead into the underbrush.

For beyond the fence there are small saplings and twisting vines. Then comes the pine forest, its trees growing tall and straight in carefully formed rows. There are angles of green between the brown trunks, since no one has cleared out this area in more than twenty years. Maples and dogwoods grow between the pines, reaching out and through the dark bodies for a slender piece of sun.

I'm careful as I step over fallen logs and broken limbs. Even though I've never said so out loud, when I walk in these woods I always consider the mother of the snakes that I stepped on, the snakes that bit me. I'm troubled that she might still be aware of my trespassing and continue—even now, so many years later—to search for the one who disrupted her home.

Burlap looks for purple-tailed lizards but doesn't get too far away from me. He dances through the thick underbrush and emerges with his tail wagging and his tongue fallen to the side of his mouth. He loves to go through this forest and down across the meadow; and I wonder if he ever ventures this path alone. He seems, like me, to come beyond the borders of our yard only when he travels with a companion.

Beyond the pines there's a cleared section, a

meadow that grows tall with cornflowers, heather, and bleeding hearts, now dormant, and bears small pink violets, like buttons, on fat green stems. It's lined on all four sides with clusters of blackberry bushes and honeysuckle. I walk to the edge to see how the berries are forming and notice that the bushes are weeks away from yielding the sugary black fruit.

The other vines are blooming, however, and the entire meadow is still fringed in a sweet, hypnotic bouquet. When I get to the middle of the open space, I find myself a small, even piece of ground and lay down. Burlap hurries through the yellow-brown stalks to curve himself next to me, and together we soak in this brief taste of summer.

The sun is high and motionless, and I watch the clouds, bounding and full, flex and lengthen with the whim of every wind. I linger, bathing in the fragrance and restfulness, until soon my eyes grow heavy and close; and before I realize it, I'm deep into the dream from my thirteenth year—that one I had the night before I had my first period.

Unlike the muddy waters of my snake night-mares, the sea this dream puts me in is clear; its waters are deep blue and brimming with harmless life. I need not worry about lungs or air, for I'm held fast, like a baby, in this depth; and I swim slow and long into the wide vastness of this ocean.

I glide by white stones and coarse, moving stars that roll along the floor. I stop to rest in the dimpled arms of a long, ancient cave of coral, sitting like a queen in heaven. I join a school of red and yellow fish that swim in time, as if one large animal. Together we sail through the waters left, then right, then straight ahead, always effortlessly.

Just as I slow down to feel the swaying grass and cup my hands to catch the gold as the rocks peel off in glimmering flecks, I become aware of the nearness of another creature. The school goes on without me as I turn to see who feels so close. And here, in the flurry of the school's passing, I'm joined by a great silver dolphin. She glides beside me so gently that it seems as if she's a part of me. Leaning her fin into me, like a

❦

handshake, she greets me. I take the fin and she pulls me slowly, then faster, through the water. It feels like we're flying.

I lose all the skins that hold me in, all the layers of my silent desires and disappointments; and I push through the sapphire blue and the salty foam and the diamond glints of light, caressed and enveloped in the idea that I can move so fast, so far, and so freely. And just before I emerge from the blueness into the air for breath and flight and into the orange brightness that I know I've dreamed before, a shadow moves across the surface of the water and I'm awakened by Burlap's bark of surprise.

"Hey," a voice calls from that same shadow.

I stir to shake off sleep, but my mind remains full of webs.

Burlap jumps up and the shadow drops to rest on haunches while patting and scratching my dog. I sense a face close to mine, but I'm still to groggy to focus. I recognize something about the shadow and yet not. Whatever that something is, it seems old or forgotten or not quite developed.

"You're the one who went off the road to keep from hitting that deer," the voice says, as if offering an answer to a quiz.

I nod, trying to sit up, but the nap and the buzzing in my head keep me leaning on one elbow a bit longer. Finally I'm able to lift myself into a sitting position.

The shadow, now clearly a man, appears to notice my dizziness, so he asks, "You all right?"

I don't reply.

"I mean from the blow and all." He touches his own forehead.

I don't have a bandage anymore, but my brow is still swollen and bruised and there are little strips of tape holding the skin together. I'm sure my forehead looks like a fat, black-stained pillow with a jagged silver seam running across.

"Oh, yeah, I'm okay," I say, studying his features. "Yeah," I repeat.

I squint and blink in an effort to remember who he is.

"Nice out here," he says. "This your land?"

I shake my head; and when he turns to look at me again, blue dissolves around him, a shade unrolls somewhere inside my mind, and the sun spreads across my memories.

"You're Sterling," I say, half-asking, half-remembering.

"Uh-huh," he says. Then he looks at me a bit suspiciously, like he wonders how I know his name.

"You were there, when it happened." Things are feeling clearer. "You looked in the car."

"Right before you threw up," he adds.

Now I'm embarrassed. Not all remembering needs to be talked about out loud.

"Don't worry about it," he says. "Daddy's seen worse." Then he sits down and Burlap rushes into his lap.

"Your daddy a preacher?" I ask, wondering when a minister would have seen worse. The most I've ever known a preacher to get dirty is when there's a baptism right after rain and the creek gets all muddy and high.

"He works at an old-folks' home to make money. Ain't no salary in preaching." Sterling whistles a bit to Burlap.

"He's helped a lot of sick people," he says.

"He got one old woman to walk after she'd been in a wheelchair for thirty years; and they said he brought Humphrey Natchez back from the dead."

Then he shrugs his shoulders like maybe it doesn't matter. "He's done a lot of stuff like that," he adds.

"Y'all from Nevada?" I ask, thinking of the license plate on the trailer.

He looks up, interested. "Yeah, up near Idaho." He waits a minute. "How did you know we were from Nevada?"

"I saw your camper that morning of the accident. I read your tags."

He makes a humming noise like he's thinking. While he's preoccupied, I'm able to focus on his graceful shoulders and the ease of his face and his long, gentle fingers.

He's as golden as honey, this boy everybody thought was Jesus. His skin is freckled from the sun, and he glistens with a light summer sweat. His eyes are brown, like loam. And though there's no blue or green or liquid edge about him, sitting here with him reminds me curiously of the ocean I've just swam.

He looks away just at the moment I realize I've been staring. I look away too.

"I wonder what time it's getting to be," I say, trying to push aside this crookedness that's come between us.

I start to get up just as he rises. He looks at his watch. "It's about three," he replies.

I take a swallow of water from my bottle and hold it out, offering him a drink. He takes the bottle from me, casually brushing his fingers across mine. Something leaps inside of me like a frog off a leaf and I feel my face start to go red.

He turns the bottle up for a drink; and as he does, I notice the long line of his neck and the short, rhythmic movements of his throat, opening and closing. The movements are slow and in time, like the start of a Spanish dance. And right then I decide that his throat is the most splendid thing I've ever seen.

He hands me back the bottle, which is now almost empty. "Thanks," he says, running his lips over each other.

"We're staying over at the other end of the lake," he says. "Daddy likes to fish." He stops

147

like he's said too much, then reaches down and rubs Burlap on the head.

With his face turned away from me, his neck bowed and low, his shoulders round and hunched, he offers, "You can join us for supper if you like."

We stand in silence a few minutes while I'm trying to understand the frogs and flies that have gotten loose in my stomach and wondering whether or not I should be traipsing across these woods with a boy I don't know. And it's a surprise to myself when I hear the word *okay* slip out of my mouth.

Sterling lifts up and looks me briefly in the eyes. He nods and heads towards the creek.

As he takes my hand to walk across the path, into and back out of the creekbed, then around through the narrow opening to the north side of the lake, I wonder when he found this abandoned trail. I wonder how close he's come to the back of our house and whether or not he's ever been in the breeze and the light that tumble through my open window.

I wonder how many times he's lumbered

through the vines and the forest and the clear open meadow. But I don't ask him, and I'm not offended that he leads me as if I've never come this way. Even after we're out in the open, I still feel the print of his strong, curled hand—the hand that rested in mine and guided me over limbs and around stones and through ditches.

Down at the second-to-the-last campsite, Reverend Renfrow has backed his Nevada Airstream into the space so that the morning sun comes through his front window instead of the back. I suppose it will also be quicker to leave, if he ever needs to be gone in a hurry. But I don't know what his plans are for Pleasant Cross and Sterling. Six days ago I wouldn't have cared, but today, for reasons I can't explain, I feel the need to know.

"Daddy?" Sterling calls, knocking on the door while looking out around the lake. He turns back to me like he wasn't sure I'd still be here.

There's a stirring in the trailer, a burst of sound, some movement. Just then the door opens and there stands the biggest, darkest man I've ever seen. He looks as giant as a bear; but when he sees me, he softens and smiles and drops down on the first step so that he doesn't appear so harsh.

"Well, Lord bless us. Look who's come across our path once again." He reaches out his enormous hand and pulls me inside with one long and easy tug. He's been cooking, and it smells like dinner. Sterling waits, then comes in behind me.

"You got yourself a pretty good bump there, young lady." Reverend Renfrow backs up and pulls out a chair at the small kitchen table, then sits down beside me. Sterling goes into the adjoining room.

"How did you find us?" he asks. While I look for my voice, he gets up and gathers three glasses from a tray by the sink, along with a plastic pitcher of lemonade, and begins to pour without asking if I want a drink.

He sets my lemonade down right in front of me and I take several swallows. Then I set the glass back on the table and lick my lips.

"She was out in the meadow, near the creek," Sterling says, answering for me as he walks into the kitchen. Then he takes his glass and drinks it all down. I study his throat again, his beautiful, rhythmic throat.

"We live over on that side," I explain.

My eyes follow Sterling as he takes a seat in an old rocking chair in the corner. Then I turn and glance around the inside of the trailer. There's cabbage boiling in a big pot on the stove. I know because the smell is strong, and it fills the tiny space. The oven bulb is on, and I see a pan on the rack in the middle. It's hot in the Airstream, even with all the windows open and a big fan running on high. But it's lovely in this space, all filled up with the things of men.

There's fishing gear stuck in all the corners and along tops of counters. There are lures and hooks of various sizes sitting about, and bright plastic worms that are feathered in lavender and pink. Men's socks and shoes are heaped by the door, while an oversized coat and three baseball caps rest on hangers on the door's backside. The walls are bare except for a picture of Moses, the prophet, near the sofa and a plaque of the Ten Commandments on the wall in front of the table.

No curtains on the windows, just small aluminum blinds that I'm sure came with the trailer when it was new.

Even above the pungent odor of the stewed cabbage, the trailer smells like men too. The heavy scents of sandalwood and musk that are mixed together in men's shaving lotion and cologne. A deep and woodsy scent, like birch leaves, that I noticed on Sterling. The dishes in the sink are chipped and faded, and the glasses we're drinking from are old jelly jars that have been washed clean. The tablecloth is hard and worn, and the seats have been taped over with broad silver tape, suggesting tears beneath.

It's a man's dwelling and appears to have been so for a very long time.

"Well, welcome to our humble abode." The Reverend drops his hands in his lap and lets me look around some more.

"I do hope you're hungry, because supper is already cooking," he says.

I think it's a little early for the evening meal, but I feel like I could eat.

"Sterling, will you check the fire out back to

see if it's hot enough to fry the fish?" The Reverend stands up and opens the small refrigerator, pulling out a plate of scaled, cut, and breaded fish—brim and crappies, I think. He puts them on the table. They're mostly small, but I'm sure they're fresh, since through the window I can see a picnic table still covered with newspaper and fish heads.

Sterling stands up from his seat in the rocker and walks out the door. As he leaves, he looks in my direction. I smile and turn away.

Reverend Renfrow is stirring the cabbage and twirling a toothpick in his mouth with his tongue.

"I'd like to tell you how much I appreciate what you did for me the morning of the accident," I say, wiping the sweat from the glass of lemonade with a paper towel I find on the table. "I don't know how Mama would have gotten me to the hospital without you."

"Oh, hush now, Baby," he says, like he's known me for a long time. He puts the lid back on the pot and hands me the plate of fish. "The Lord wanted me to help you, and that's just what I did. Now how about taking this out to the boy to start cooking? I'll be out there in a minute. I just need to fix the salad."

It seems funny to me that everything is so ready, so prepared. It's almost as if he knew I was coming. And just as I think this, he winks at me as if he recognizes what I'm thinking. I suppose I've never spent a lot of time imagining such, but there must be others who have a gift of Knowing too. Reverend Renfrow pulls out vegetables from a grocery bag at my side and laughs like I've been talking out loud.

Then I remember my assignment and take the plate outside to a small campfire that Sterling is leaned over and arranging. I see a large frying pan on the picnic table, next to some bacon grease in a coffee can, so I deliver them too, nudging Sterling on the shoulder with the handle of the pan.

He turns and lifts up his chin in a nod, then sets the pan beside him and reaches for the can of grease. Sticking his fingers in, he pulls out a huge dollop of white animal fat and flips it in the pan, which I then place on the charcoal. He wipes his hand first on his jeans and then on a handkerchief he's got in his back pocket. After a couple of minutes he takes the fish, tail by tail, and drops them in the popping grease.

I go inside to get a fork or a spatula to turn the fish and see Reverend Renfrow cracking open a head of lettuce. He motions towards the cooking utensils before I even ask, winking at me again.

I back out of the trailer and hand Sterling the fork. "Your Daddy read people's minds?" I ask.

Sterling flips a couple pieces of fish before answering. "I guess so," he says, " 'cept he calls it the Lord talking to him." He pushes the fish with the fork. "He's always been that way, ever since I been with him."

I think it's odd that Sterling uses those words—"been with him"—instead of saying something like "as long as I been born" or "all my life." It almost sounds like Reverend Renfrow isn't really his father or something, but I expect it wouldn't be very cordial of me to ask such a thing on our first official meeting.

I'm guessing that we'll be eating outside, since there were only two chairs at the table inside and since it's so hot in there. So I go over and start wrapping up the fish guts and heads in the paper and wipe away the scales and slime that have soaked through. Burlap is under my feet, so I throw a fish head away from the table and watch him run to pick it up. He holds it in his mouth and turns back to the woods, his tail wagging, probably off to bury his prize.

Reverend Renfrow makes a couple of trips bringing out the salad and cabbage, plates, and other things, whistling and singing as he does. And after I throw away the trash, I go back in to get the other stuff left on the table. On the way out, my arms loaded down with dressing and napkins and silverware, I notice a picture of Reverend Renfrow, a woman, and a small child. It's in a frame that's pushed to the back of a shelf behind a tackle box. Putting down the bottle of dressing to free up a hand, I pull out the picture so I can see better.

Reverend Renfrow, young here but still large and looming, is holding a Bible, tucked at his wrist on his right side. His left arm is awkwardly placed around the shoulders of a young

black girl with her hip thrown out and a golden
baby boy—Sterling, I believe—resting upon it.
The picture is old and dusty, but I'm still able to
see the girl's tense appearance, her body facing
the photographer but her chin and eyes angled
to the small boy crouched into her. He's holding
the pendent on her necklace—a cross, it looks
like—tugging at it so that the chain is taut and
biting into her skin.

The Reverend is the only one smiling, but his
turned-up lips look out of place and rehearsed.
The picture was taken in front of a small
wooden church, and there are people gathered
at the front steps watching the action of the photograph. One woman stands slightly between
the building and the threesome and seems to be
trying to get out of the way. All of the women
are dressed in hats and high heels, lovely spring
dresses; and the men are in sharp tailored suits
that even in this faded picture appear expensive
and new.

As I trace my eyes across the picture, I'm
drawn back to the girl who's holding the child.
Since she's turned away at the moment the cam-

era clicks, it's hard to see her features, but there's something strangely familiar about her. She's not particularly striking, not extraordinarily beautiful, though there's a pleasant youthfulness about her. She looks sixteen or so, and it looks as if the photograph and this church and this large Bible-holding man have been set before her against the desires of her heart.

I hear Sterling and Reverend Renfrow moving towards the picnic table, so I put down the picture, pick back up the bottle of salad dressing, and hurry out the door. They're setting out plates and plastic forks and spoons and arranging the bowls and dishes of food in the center of the table. Sterling goes back inside to bring out our glasses, the pitcher, and salt and pepper while Reverend Renfrow takes up the fish from the fire, kicks a little sand on the charcoal, and places the pan on a stack of dishtowels at the end of the table. We all sit down.

Reverend Renfrow folds his hands together and bows his head. Sterling looks exactly the same, as I know I should, but I'd rather watch the two of them than close my eyes to pray.

❧

"O Lord, Creator of earth and sky, we bless your holy name for this feast we are about to receive. We bless you for the fish that nourish us today, the vegetables from your bountiful earth, and the fresh, clean juice of lemons that fills us with delight."

Sterling is so still. With his head down, I can see the tiny knots of hair cut short and fine. I can see the tips of his earlobes and three drops of sweat trickling down his neck. I can see his chin resting upon his chest and the sharp, narrow thrust of his collarbone. I can see the interlacing of his fingers and remember how they felt inside mine; and I can see the thin, dark lines that separate his arms from his hands. I can see his knuckles and his ivory nails and . . .

"We thank you, Lord, for our guest, for her health and well being and her pleasure in being with us."

I snap my eyes shut.

"Lead, guide, and direct us now, we pray. Amen."

I lift my head and smile at the preacher and his son as if I'm pleased with his blessing.

Then this remarkable meal begins. The cabbage is seasoned with just enough pork, its taste strong and meaty. The cornbread, homemade, is studded with tiny pieces of jalapeño peppers and whole kernels of silver-white corn. The salad is fresh and firm and chock-full of vine-ripe red tomatoes and new, just-picked cucumbers; and the fish is so tender it melts in my mouth. The lemonade is sweet, with real slices of lemon swimming at the tops of our glasses.

The food more than satisfies my hunger; it lifts up a longing I didn't even know was there and settles me in an unannounced completeness. As I savor delicious bites and lengthy, slow swallows, I feel myself stretch inside from the delight in my mouth and the airy sensation swelling up in my chest.

A breeze rustles in the trees and cools the top of my head and the bottoms of my feet. The sun splits and splinters into shining rays that push and pull through clouds and limbs and diverge around large gray birds that glide high above us before diving straight down into the deep, green lake. The sky is a palette of blues, heavy and wisped; and the play of darkness and lightness adds to the rising up and flowing over of my cup.

Reverend Renfrow doesn't say a word. He laughs at my seeing, my eating and enjoying. He touches me on the arm, then looks at his son, nodding his head as if he's arranged everything I am, everything I'm feeling. But I don't care about what he Knows or doesn't know. I'm dizzy or drunk or just plain happy; and I doubt that I'll ever feel so content and untangled again.

The tastes, the smells, the textures and colors and sounds from the lake, and the wonderment and ease and arrival of this boy—this beautiful, shy, simple, honey-toned boy—creates for me the notion that heaven does, once in awhile, when you're really paying attention, or graced in the company of generous people, tenderly place its mark upon you.

Such joy, pure and undeniable joy, has suddenly found itself in me that it's easy to see how I might miss the signs of the coming storm forming around us. Mama says that pleasure has a way of denying the presence of trouble. But as I look about us now, I notice the subtle changes in the sky.

I know that I've studied enough of Grandma's ways to understand the summer season. I can't predict the clouds days in advance like she can; and I don't name whether it's wind or rain or hail that a storm will bring. But I've watched with her at so many dawns and dusks and twilights that I've picked up shapes and warnings that speak of what's to come.

So far, this is what I've learned. At first, there's a question mark angled in the sky, a gesture of consideration, a tilt towards the possibility. Then the clouds move closer together as if they share a common thought or idea. They bunch and gather. The breezes gain a stiffness, a sting; and the leaves on maple trees flip inside out, disclosing a pointed silver belly.

Birds suddenly disappear, hiding in cloaks of thick, crowded bushes, and the ears on dogs stand straight up as if someone were approaching. A smell of clean wash drifts about, and blades of grass gradually bend and roll like waves in the sea.

As I slowly begin to read these signs around this picnic table of bounty, and as we sit in silence, I lift my nose into the air and take in a deep breath. "A storm is coming," I say.

Reverend Renfrow takes in a similar breath, holding his great chin up towards the sky, and bellows out the word "yes" that sounds deep and old.

Sterling closes his eyes and follows our example. When he opens them, he just whispers, "Amen."

And that was the best prayer I ever prayed.

We clean up the dishes, not hurriedly or in excitement but in a way that lends respect to nature and the rain that's fast approaching. When we're finished stacking and cleaning, Reverend Renfrow sends us out before the darkened sky splits open. He hands Sterling the keys to the truck and takes both of my hands in his. "We'll see each other again soon," he says.

I nod in agreement.

I climb into the truck while Sterling whistles for Burlap, then holds open the gate to the covered flatbed so that the dog can jump in. Then Sterling pulls the gate up and locks it in place with the top hatch. As he gets in the driver's side, large drops of rain begin to fall. They land like puddles on the front of the truck and on his back, and I lean forward to look up into the sky. Reverend Renfrow is standing at the door waving to us with a grin as big as a river.

Sterling backs out onto the lake road slowly, then turns right to get to the main highway. Neither of us speaks. I try not to look at him, but I keep turning to my left to catch one more glimpse of his cheek or to memorize how he bites his lip or how he holds the steering wheel with one hand, the grip tight and careful. "Make the second right into the park," I say, without even looking at the road.

He turns the truck into the driveway, then flips on his lights and windshield wipers because the rain is coming harder and faster. I look ahead. As I point out our house, I see Liddy standing on the porch with the phone cord stretched from the kitchen and out the door. She goes in and hangs up when she sees us drive up.

Sterling gets out just as I do and we meet at the back, where he opens the gate and lets Burlap out. The dog jumps from the truck and runs under the house, but we simply stand there looking at each other. I hardly notice the rain that's soaking us, the thunder that's shaking the earth, or the lightning firing up the sky. I can't shape words to invite him in or ask him to come by later or thank him for dinner or tell him that it was good to see him. I can't think *what* to say.

Then, with his left arm still holding up the top of the gate at the back of the truck, he leans towards me and places his lips on mine. The kiss is quick and loose and melts me like a flame. He pulls away and closes the hatch while I remain motionless, caught in this surprise.

"Can I see you?" he asks politely, shyly.

Still tingling, my heart pounding like a jackhammer, I nod a yes. I hear a door slam on our front porch and remember Liddy. "Um, tomorrow?" I ask.

"Yes," he says.

Then I walk around him to the edge of the porch and stand there, still uncovered in the rain, and wait until he's backed out, pulled away, and driven out of sight.

I feel Liddy come up behind me. "Give me your hand" is all that she says.

5

The Bank of Sandy Creek

✻ There was no *R* in my palm. Liddy had me turn my hands one way and then the other, wash with sage soap, spit on them, and hold them above a silver-tipped candle; but the best she could come up with was an upright line with a hook at the end. There was no intersection of three lines leading to the formation of a round and open *R*. As hard as my sister tried, Sterling Renfrow couldn't be located within the secrets held in my hand.

I told her that it didn't matter, that maybe she's wrong once in awhile; and I was even willing to try to make myself believe that what I said was true. But everybody knows that she's never missed. Liddy's reading is the final seal of approval for any engagement and the assurance needed for any doubtful or tentative mate. And for those who've defied her reading, divorce or breakup has always followed.

I've decided, however, not to allow this brutal comment on my love life to alter my desires or intentions one bit. I'm going to ask for and take all that I can get. I'm not going to stop myself by thinking or planning or looking for signs. I'm already fully headlong into the ocean of this bliss.

I love Sterling Renfrow. I don't know how it happened or the exact moment it happened or even if it's happened to him. I don't know and I don't care. He's the burning hub my world spins around. And even if Liddy is right in the end and what we have can't last, I'll twist and dance around the light that reflects off his memory until it's taken away.

I love how his eyes are earth-rich brown like the space in my garden where only good things grow. I love how he fidgets any time he's inside and how he loosens and becomes unknotted once he gets outdoors. I love the clean and definite shape of his mouth and his long narrow feet. I love how he'll gently lift a ladybug and hold it ever so lightly on the tip of his finger until the tiny insect grows weary, releases her hidden wings, and flies away.

I love how he looks at his father with favor and how he recognizes the tracks of wild turkeys and honors the flight of the red-winged hawk. I love the way he saunters through briars and brush and vines of poison without ever noticing the damage that could be done.

I love the strength of his calm, sturdy hands and the cool invitation that he offers with his smile. I love his silent, thinking manner and the meek and humble way he lowers himself to pray. I love the possibilities and the mysteries and the hurrying up to wait and see. I love everything about this boy and his father and the stretch of joy I feel right now. So I'm not at all concerned or put out that my sister doesn't Know that this is destined. There are, in my opinion, some things even more reliable than my family's ways of Knowing. And loving Sterling Renfrow is the best of these.

꒰꓄

Sterling and I have seen each other every day since that afternoon I fell asleep in the meadow and we kissed in the rain. That was one week and three days ago. On Thursday of last week we met again in the meadow and talked of wild horses and dead trees that remain standing and the places in the creek where stones are smooth and etched with fossils of tadpoles. We walked all the way from the lake to Hasty's Store for Pepsi and peanuts and then back, way behind the fields.

Friday he came over to the house and helped me weed the garden and rebuild the trellis for my Joseph's Coat rosebush. I made sandwiches while he played with Burlap, and then we had lunch in a small clearing in the pine-tree forest, hemmed in by trunks of trees and tight yellow flowers.

Saturday afternoon we fished with the Reverend and ate a bucket of cherries that we'd picked that morning. Sunday we went to revival services at AME Zion Church, just over the border in Alamance County. Afterwards we sat on the ground eating plates of barbecue and ham salad and sharing a bowl of homemade pecan-cluster ice-cream.

On our long, lazy days together we spoke of wars and spiders and the differences between dreams and wishes. We compared the size of our knees and made necklaces from swan-river daisies. We discussed baseball and having children and how to graft bark rootstocks. And we bathed in easy flowing bouts of silence when we didn't need to say a thing.

We could spend the whole day together and it wouldn't be nearly enough. I smell him everywhere—on my clothes, in my pockets, along the tips of my fingers. I taste him. I dream him. He's leaped across my path and been driven, like a bolt of lightning, into my heart. And Mama and Liddy can look at me all they want, with those hard sideways looks, and I don't even care. What's done is done. The falling has already passed.

Even though I went back to work on Monday, I've still been seeing Sterling regularly. He doesn't like to go inside restaurants, but he's come for lunch every day. He's had meatloaf, grilled cheese, Salisbury steak, and chicken pie; and one day he ordered the chef's salad just because he'd never had one. Yesterday, Friday, he had spaghetti, and I watched from the small oval window in the kitchen door as he twirled the noodles around his fork. He makes everything look delicious.

Luther gives me a rough time about it since I haven't ever had a boy coming in to see me. He says things like, "You better make sure you can cook, because that boyfriend of yours eats more than two men," or "You better find yourself somebody else; he don't even leave you a fifty-cent tip."

But I don't pay him any mind. I have a difficult enough time listening to the other customers and remembering whether they want their dressing on the side or poured over the top of their lettuce or whether they said Coke or tea. My eyes are so stuck on Sterling Renfrow that I can hardly see anything or anybody else.

The first day he came in, I spilled orange juice all over the Colemans' table. Luckily, the little girl, Prissy, had been acting up, so they thought she'd had something to do with it. I apologized and all, but they still made her sit down in the booster chair and be in time-out.

Then I got Mr. Davis's order wrong. He'd wanted chicken-fried steak and I wrote down chicken fillet. But again it worked out to my needs, because he decided the sandwich and french fries looked better than the meat plate anyway. So nobody has yet to catch on that I've been so distracted I can't remember the special and have to keep reading it off the board.

Well, no, Reverend Renfrow knows. He's come in every noon with Sterling. And he seems amused by the whole thing. Of course, that just makes me more jumpy. But after I saw him bow his head that first day at Luther's, then lift up his chin like it was the end of his prayer, I felt more steady. I didn't drop any more glasses or get an order wrong after that. Given how set he seems on me and Sterling finding our ways to each other, I wonder what he'd say about my sister not uncovering his son's name in the lines of my hand.

This evening I'm walking to the lake to meet

Sterling, and we're driving over to Cordessa's for the big Fourth of July cookout. Mama didn't say a word yesterday when I told her I was going. She gathered up her face in a mass of wrinkles and looked like she was going to yell something fierce, but then she turned up the volume on the TV and gave me her back, pretending not to hear me and Liddy talking about what I was going to wear.

I decided on the bib overalls I bought at Goody's last month, along with a midriff shirt that looks sort of like a bandanna. Neither Liddy nor me is very chesty, but since I'll be covered in the overalls I don't mind wearing something a little tighter than usual.

Liddy never seems to worry about her flatness. She's even been known to see it as a good thing. She said once that at least we could always be confident that boys weren't interested in us just for our tits. And she's always pranced around unashamed to show what she has.

I, on the other hand, have always felt a bit self-conscious, like maybe I should wear a padded bra or big billowy shirts. Because of it, I'm a little hunched over and keep my arms folded across me a lot. Liddy made me buy the midriff shirt and has convinced me that it really does look sexy, even though I feel like a twelve-year-old in it.

I leave a few minutes early because I got ready quicker than I thought and nobody else is home to talk to. Mama hasn't gotten back from the grocery store, and Liddy had to be at work early this morning. Burlap chases me out the back and hurries ahead, already sure of where we're going.

I walk through the pine-tree forest, out into the meadow, and over along the bank of the Sandy Creek. I notice a car heading down towards the widening place at the narrow body of water, the place where the old fishing shack still stands; and I remember the sight of Mama and the preacher and wonder if I should go down there to see if the future has merged into the present. But I realize that it would take me an extra twenty minutes to get there and back; and besides, what good would it do to verify what I already Know?

Lynne Hinton

I have to walk along the creek to the old log bridge because the rain has filled the shallow bed and I don't want to get wet. As I slog through the brush to the south side of the lake, I see Reverend Renfrow sitting at the water's edge fishing. He notices me as I come into the clearing.

"Happy Fourth of July to you, Baby," he says, sounding glad to see me.

"Happy Fourth of July to you, Reverend Renfrow." Burlap runs up to him. "Anything biting?"

"Just the gnats," he replies with his big ol' grin.

"You been here all day?" I ask.

"No, no. I had some business to tend to in town," he says, fiddling with his line and looking more serious than I've ever seen him.

"Oh," I say. Then, since I haven't known him to have any business in town before, I ask, "What kind of business?"

"At the Baptist church," he says, "with the Reverend Thurman Lawson." Then he looks at me expectantly.

❧

"That's *our* church," I say.

"Yes," he agrees, drawing it out like there's more.

"You planning on preaching there?" I squat down next to him and look towards the trailer to see if I can see Sterling.

"Perhaps," he says, all shadowy. "One never knows what the Lord has in mind."

Then he sees me watching the Airstream. "The boy is getting ready," he says. "He should be out in a few minutes."

I nod and turn towards the lake. The sun is lowering, and a large shadow falls across the water.

"Where is it y'all are going?" he asks.

"It's just a bar on the outskirts of town. My sister works there." I tug on his line a bit and he winks at me, having seen what I've done.

"There's a cookout," I say. After a minute I look up at him and add, "You're welcome to join us."

"Cordessa Gordon's place?" He seems almost reluctant to ask for details.

"Pender," I say. "Cordessa Pender." Burlap runs

to the trailer. I hear a door shut and see Sterling coming around the corner.

"Cordessa Pender," the Reverend repeats. And then he goes all quiet, his face and shoulders slumped.

"You know her?" Watching Sterling walk towards us, I don't hear what Reverend Renfrow says, if he answers. I'm looking at how Sterling moves across the grass, how tall he seems, how good I know he's going to smell. He comes to stand right beside me.

"Y'all be careful tonight," Reverend Renfrow says, coughing. "It's always more dangerous to be out on a holiday."

"Yes, sir," we both say, not paying him much attention.

I get up to join Sterling, then we turn and walk back towards the trailer. Burlap runs ahead, but I send him back to the lake. When I turn around to watch the dog's happy trot, I see that the Reverend has put the pole on the ground beside him and has dropped his face in his hands. I stop and touch Sterling on the arm, as if we might should turn around; but as if he's seen us, Reverend Renfrow pulls his head up and smiles in our direction, waving us on our way. Burlap stations himself at his side.

Sterling noticed him too. "Just praying, I reckon." He reaches out and takes my hand. I love the way we walk like this, hand in hand, even when we're not climbing over rocks or forging our way through briars.

We get in the truck and drive to Cordessa's. He pulls me closer to him on the slippery seat so that our legs touch, and I realize that we really are a couple. And we're going out in public for the first time, where people will meet us and learn us as one distinct being.

"This is Tessa and Sterling," Liddy will say as she introduces us around.

"Tessa and Sterling, I'd like you to meet So-and-so," others will say.

And I'm not pressed down by it, or confused or unhappy that something has now changed and I'm a part of someone else. I like it; and as we pull into the driveway and park, I touch him on the face and he turns to me and we kiss.

Then he brushes the back of his hand across

my cheek and smiles at me. "Daddy likes you," he says.

"I like him too. He's very nice."

"He says God put us together, like the lake and the sun."

"What do *you* say?" I ask, pulling myself around to face him.

"I say I haven't ever talked to anybody like you before."

Though I'm a bit embarrassed by the weight of our conversation, I don't want to quit.

"We don't have to go if you don't want to," I say, causing the mood to shift a bit.

"No, we should go," he says, pulling out his keys. "Your sister will be happy."

He opens his door and gets out, then holds out his hand as I slide over.

We head straight through the crowded bar to an area behind the building that's been decorated with streamers and flags and huge banners in red, white, and blue. Liddy is standing near an outdoor grill serving burgers and hotdogs and minding the condiment table. She doesn't see us when we walk out.

❧

We stop and take in what's going on around us. A band is playing, and lots of people are standing in small groups and talking. I reach down to feel for Sterling's hand.

We walk over to where Liddy is working, and when she sees us she reaches around the grill and gives us both a big hug.

"Hey, I'm so glad you're here!" she says, handing over plates and hamburger buns. "Isn't this great? Cordessa says it's already the biggest crowd she's ever had."

"Yeah?" I ask, opening my bun to put mustard and ketchup on it. "You working hard?"

"Oh, it's been crazy. But I'm having a good time—making good tips," she adds, smiling.

"Sterling, you like it out here in the country?" she asks. She takes two burgers off the grill and plops them on our plates.

"It's what I'm used to," he says. He fixes his hamburger and pours some chips next to it.

"Yeah, well, it might be what I'm used to too, but I'm looking forward to city life!" She puts some more burgers on a platter. "I'm heading to Albuquerque!"

❧

She arranges the burgers with her spatula. "Cordessa's is about the only thing good I can think of around these parts." Then she puts the plate down and looks at me, " 'Cept my little sister, of course," she says, laughing.

We move away from the table to get out of other people's way. "Don't go too far," she calls to us. "I want you to say hey to Cordessa."

We walk around until we find a place to sit down. We eat and listen to the music without talking much to each other or to anyone else. It's a local band, blues and beach music, mostly. A few people are dancing.

The crowd is a nice blend, black and white, old and young, a lot of families. I recognize some folks as I look around, but not enough to go over and make conversation. Sterling gets up to get a beer since he's of age and to find me a can of Mountain Dew. While he's gone I try to see if there are any other couples that look like us—a black boy and a white girl. I don't see any.

Now, it isn't that this is of any concern to *me*; matters of race never have been. But it dawned on me recently that this might not be the average thing. That in addition to being from the Ivy family, which already carries a certain taint, the fact that I'm dating a black boy—a golden boy, a creamy coffee boy—might add another few feet to the gully that separates me and Liddy and Mama and Doris and Grandma from the rest of Pleasant Cross.

I'm not the first Ivy to date outside our own race. Doris shacked up with an Indian man named Nigel who played pool for a living. He hung around a few months until somebody he hustled got after him. Then he left without ever letting Doris know how to find him. Neither Grandma nor Mama ever said anything bad about Nigel or the color of his skin, except a comment about having him walk up on them at twilight one evening and being able to see only the white of his eyes.

Seems to me most of my family is downright color-blind, and that's the way I like it. Sterling's soul is held in by that sun-touched skin, but just like me in my peach-fuzz whiteness, he isn't confined by it.

Grandma said one time after Jasper starting

going out with Cordessa's daughter, Millie, "Matters of the heart are much too weighty to be determined by outside appearances. You start judging who you're going to love by the color of their skin or the percentage of their body fat," she said, "and you'll almost certainly lose something in the end."

That's part of the reason they haven't said too much about Sterling and the fact that he isn't white. Grandma favored him right away, said he had a gentleness about him that made him feel like family. Doris said he was fine as muskmelon wine, and Liddy told me she'd already searched her palm to make sure he hadn't gotten us mixed up.

Only Mama is a little distant with Sterling. I haven't quite figured that out yet. I'm sure it doesn't have to do with how he looks or the fact that he's living out of a camping trailer, since she's never had a problem with pride. But it's like she gets sort of squint-eyed when he's around, like she's sniffing him, hounding him, trying to find out something hidden.

He hasn't seemed to notice, or at least he hasn't said anything. But *I've* noticed, and it occurs to me suddenly that it might have something to do with the busted friendship and the Reverend and all that stuff floating in my tea.

Just as I'm thinking this and considering the idea that I might be on to something, Cordessa comes outside with a huge pot of chili in her hands, ordering people out of her way and pushing through the crowd like she's parting the Red Sea.

Medium-sized and clear-eyed, she's as brown as burnt toast. She's still young—same age as Mama, I guess, late thirties. And I can see how she seems part girlish and part middle-aged woman. I suppose I haven't seen her since Millie's funeral five or six years ago. She looks the same, only a little darker and a little deeper in thought.

As she gets closer, hurrying past me, I notice that she leans to the left with her hip, like that's the strongest part of her body. And when she gets to the table and sets the pot down, she wipes her forehead with the same arm that's cradled more than one lost baby. I see that her glances still hint of some long-ago pain.

I realize from some yards away, without a strike or quiver of any Ivy sign of Knowing, that Cordessa is the woman in the photograph in the Airstream. I'm sure beyond any need for verification. And then, like putting the pieces of a puzzle together, I suddenly understand that Reverend Renfrow has come to Pleasant Cross to reunite Sterling with his mother. That he even understood that the reunion would happen tonight.

I swallow my breath. I don't like the way this whole situation lays on my back. I don't like the idea of introducing Cordessa to her sent-away child or trapping Sterling into learning about his family tree. I don't like this sense that my chest is filling up with water. I decide that we should leave immediately.

When Sterling comes back with the drinks, I say that I'm not feeling well and could we please go home? We've been there only maybe an hour, so he looks at me like he's checking whether he shouldn't take me to the hospital or to my sister. But since I jump up and am able to walk over and throw away our trash, then go to Liddy and whisper something to her, he seems to believe me when I say that I just want to get away. He doesn't see Cordessa, because she's walked back into the bar and out of sight.

We ride in silence as I try to think of what I should say. I know that Reverend Renfrow thinks it's time to let his son know where he came from, but I'm not pleased to be somehow involved in this troublesome revelation. And I don't like the idea that Cordessa doesn't appear to have a say in the matter.

What was the old man thinking, just showing up like this? And why now? Why with me? I sort through the questions only to find more.

"You want to go to your house or to the trailer?" Sterling asks as we approach home.

I don't want to face Mama, and I certainly don't want to see Reverend Renfrow, so I say, "Let's go out to the creek." I remember the car that had driven on the path earlier, so I figure the way must be driveable.

As nightfall approaches like some weary guest, stars begin to appear, and suddenly I want to be out under them. We turn down the lake road and then circle back until we find the path that goes to the widest part of Sandy Creek. We drive to the edge of the water.

Sterling stops the truck and rolls down his window.

"Okay," he says, not looking at me. "You get sick or something?"

"I just needed to get away. Too many people, I guess." I pause a minute. "Do you have a blanket?"

He turns to me. "You cold?" He starts to roll up his window.

I shake my head. "To lay on," I say. "Outside, by the creek."

"Aren't you afraid of snakes?" he asks, having heard my story.

For a moment I think maybe it would be best to go home—adding snakes to this drama might be more than I can handle—but I know that this is the best place for us to be alone.

"No," I say after a long while.

He opens his door and we both get out. He goes to the back and opens the hatch to pull out a couple of blankets and, since it's getting dark, a flashlight. Then he walks around and puts one of the blankets around my shoulders and we head towards the creek.

The weeds are a bit tall here; they drag along my legs, pulling and breaking. I move a little closer to Sterling as we walk. Looking for a good spot to settle, we notice an area at the top of the creek. It appears flat and empty there, so we walk around until we find it—apparently the place where a boat used to be tied and kept. We spread out the blankets and then crawl onto them.

Sterling sits down as I settle back on my elbows, watching the moon gain position and the stars light and mingle and increase.

"The Big Dipper," he says, looking up as frogs close out a chorus.

In the night-glow of the summer sky I can see Sterling's neck, arched and stretched. I can see the unknowingness that has kept him unburdened and at ease. I can see the soft spot in his heart. I angle myself beside him and, though I don't know what I'm doing, I kiss him. Then I sit back and smile.

He stays unmoving for a few minutes, still looking up, still curved, his face blending with the sky, like he's lost in thought. Then he looks intently at me, as if I've made some proposition, and asks me if I'm sure.

I lay on my back and nod. But what confidence I've just claimed, I don't know.

I'm sure that I want no harm to come to this warmth we've uncovered within ourselves. I'm sure that I'm sore for him in a way I don't understand. I'm sure that Sterling would never hurt me. And I'm sure that I want nothing more than to protect him from the painful discovery that his mother lives only a few miles away from where he and his father have parked; and that his father knows it and I know it; but that neither of us has told him so.

He moves even closer now, one arm under my neck, the other softly touching my face, my throat. He begins to unhook my overalls, and I tremble in what I Know and what I don't know.

It's like being lost and found all at the same time—that spinning feeling that lasts even after the ride is over and your feet are touching the ground.

I'm dizzy and winded but somehow unafraid. Just as Sterling reaches beneath my shirt, touching the skin above my heart, I'm reminded of something Grandma said one time last summer after a hurricane had blown through the coast.

In the midst of the destruction, she read in the newspaper, a drug house was exposed. Clear plastic bags of cocaine and marijuana lay mixed about with picture frames and house plants, toilets and sofas. After reading about it, Grandma put down the paper and stuck yet another sunflower seed in her mouth. "Storms and love," she said, shaking her head like she was disappointed, "always squeeze out the secrets."

I put my hand over Sterling's as he gently begins to caress my breast. It's a motion to stop, and he understands. He sits up a bit, pulling his hand out from under my shirt and cupping my chin.

"Too fast?" he asks.

I lean up to kiss him, then drop my head back down. I look deep within him and feel the tears gather in my eyes.

"Baby," he says, just like the Reverend, "we don't have to do anything you don't want to."

I turn my face away from his and shake my head. We lay like that for awhile; he doesn't say a thing or move towards or away from me.

Finally, after a time of pained creekbed quiet, I have the courage to ask, "You know the picture of you when you were a baby—the one that sits on the shelf in the trailer?"

There's a long pause before he says, "The one where my mother gave me up to the preacher." He lays down beside me and waits a minute, then adds, "I'm adopted."

After another flood of quiet, he asks, "Why?"

"Did you ever know her?" I ask, turning on my side to face him now. I pull a piece of grass and roll it around in my fingers.

"No," he answers.

"Did you ever hear anything about her?"

A shooting star streams across the sky, appearing to drop just at the end of the lake, through the trees.

"Just that she was young and couldn't keep me," he says, crossing his arms and putting them behind his head. "Daddy says she wanted me close to God, so she gave me to a minister."

I stumble with the heaviness of what I know. When someone cares about another person deeply—a person in trouble—does the heart automatically drop into the stomach? Does having to say something that may be cutting or disappointing always make a person feel this rock-bottomed? Is this the falling off place that caused Mama and Grandma and Doris to make so many wrong choices in lovers?

I feel like I'm walking through the woods at midnight, no lantern, no direction, no place to go. Finally, as if I'm jumping into the deep end with my eyes closed, I just say it: "She's here." The words pour out as if of their own volition. "In Pleasant Cross."

I feel his body shift, but he doesn't move away.

"I think your dad brought you here to meet her."

He turns to the other side at that, away from me. But I go on. "It's Cordessa, at the bar."

I wait a minute before continuing. "I recognized her tonight, from the picture, and I thought I should get you out. That's why I wanted to leave." I lean up on my elbow, trying to breathe steady and trying to find his face in the darkness.

He sits up with his back towards me and I wonder with a twinge of fear what will happen next. He stays that way for a long time, until I can't distinguish the creek from the bank, the shadows from the trees. Then he gets up and offers me a hand. I stand as he picks up the blankets and the flashlight and leads me to the truck. Neither of us says anything.

He throws our stuff in the back while I get in, then jumps in beside me and starts up the truck. As we head out, he drives like he isn't angry or upset, but still he has nothing to say.

When he pulls up in our driveway, he puts the

transmission in park. After a moment he turns and pulls me toward him, into the longest, deepest kiss we've shared. Then he gets out and comes around to my side of the truck, opens the door for me.

He walks me to the porch. Mama is gone, and the house is quiet. I stop at the door. "Can't I go with you?" I ask, having no idea where he's going next.

He shakes his head and looks away. "I'll be back, though," he says to reassure me. "You know—later."

But I *don't* know, and that's what troubles me. I don't know where he's going or how long he'll be or if I should make him take me with him. I don't know anything extra.

He pulls open the screen door, then waits as I walk inside. I turn as the door swings back against me and watch him walk and then drive away, the dust and the emptiness swirling in a cloud.

When I can no longer see the lights of his car, I turn back in and notice the stillness of the house.

Mama must be gone to Grandma's or with Doris, I think—and just as I'm guessing that, I see a folded note on the counter.

L & T,

There's something I have to take care of. I'll be back sometime tomorrow.

Mom

It's odd that Mama would leave with no more of an explanation than this. She's usually much more detailed and willing to share. But frankly, the news I just delivered to Sterling and what he's planning to do with it seem a lot more important and overwhelming than my mother's untimely departure.

I get ready for bed, though I'm not sleepy, and lay down on the sofa to wait for Liddy. Maybe she knows something else about Cordessa. Maybe she has some of the answers Sterling will need tomorrow. And even though the light is still on, the door is unlocked and open, and I feel like I'm wide awake, the next thing I know I've fallen fast asleep and find myself lost in a gray and stormy dream.

The sky is blistered, dropped low and swollen tight with rain and hail. Everybody in town is running for shelter, mothers trying to hold their children beneath them and men trying to round folks up into basements and cellars. I run from person to person, house to house, trying to find something or someone familiar, but no one will help me.

Cows and fences, clocks and pocketbooks fly around me; and still I hurry, calling out for Mama or Liddy, Doris or Grandma. But I can't find the ones I love. People run around me, frantic and unhinged; the wind spins and whirls madly.

Finally, as I come to the edge of town, I see a violent funnel cloud, a compact, rolling storm that pulls and spits as it moves along its way. Bolts of lightning shoot off around it. It twirls and reels, this angry unloosed storm; and as I peer into the approaching tornado, I see Mama and Cordessa, Sterling, and a small blanketed baby being thrown about like coins in a dryer.

I stand before the reckless cloud, demanding that it stop, screaming and crying; but the weight of the wind pushes me down and I cling to the earth beneath me, my fingers digging in the dirt. I look up to see Mama being thrown from the cloud, her body slamming onto the roof of our house. Broken and lifeless, she slumps down the shingles and drops to the ground, where the baby has been thrown out and dashed below her.

Then I turn back to the storm and watch as Cordessa and Sterling, holding themselves together like lovers, fly out, end over end, and land on the steeple of the church, the large gold cross impaling the chests of both of them.

The churning cloud continues to roll across the road, over me and through me, moving from side to side, pulling up trees and cars and houses and trailers until it's blown all the way through Pleasant Cross and out the other end of town, climbing finally into the sky.

As I huddle on the ground, crying and shouting, weeping over all that's been lost and killed, someone tugs at me from above.

❧

"Tessa, Tessa, wake up!"

I watch the storm move farther and farther away, abandoning the dead bodies strewn all around me.

"Tessa, it's just a dream. Wake up!"

And I open my eyes, almost used to being interrupted now when I sleep. Aunt Doris and Grandma are standing above me. When I sit up, I see that the preacher's wife from the church is standing at the door. She looks as flushed and agitated as the people early in my dream.

"That's some nightmare you were having," Aunt Doris says, blowing smoke from her cigarette. "I'm sure you'll tell me about it." She squints at me like she's trying to read me.

"What's wrong?" I ask. "Where's Mama?" I look around them, wiping my eyes to wake up further.

"That's why we're here," Grandma says, sitting down in a rocker beside me. "Mrs. Lawson here believes your mama's run off with her husband, the preacher." Then she looks at me real hard, like I need to be careful what I say.

"I told her she was out with Deedle," Grandma

says, "gone to the beach, but she doesn't seem to believe me. So I thought maybe you could fill in the details." She's rocking in her chair.

I turn to the preacher's wife and remember the strange note that Mama left. Then I glance over at the clock, surprised to see that it's five already, just before dawn. I must have slept for several hours.

"Where's Liddy?"

"In bed over at my house. Came in a couple of hours ago because her truck broke down at the south entrance." Grandma looks like she's still waiting for me to confirm the story that will protect her daughter and my mother.

"Mrs. Lawson woke up the whole neighborhood," Aunt Doris says, sliding her hands over her hips, the cigarette balanced between her fingers. "Seems she forgot which house y'all live in."

I look over at the preacher's wife again. She's red-faced and coming undone, what with Doris's mocking manner and Grandma's unlikely suggestion. When she speaks, her voice is all high-pitched and tight. "I know she's gone off with Thurman," she says. "I just want to know where they are."

"I don't think she's with your husband," I say, trying to give credence to Grandma's story while working to get released from the storm dream I'm still enmeshed in.

"She left with Deedle—that's her brother— this morning for Emerald Isle. She gave me the phone number of where they're staying," I say, lying straight through my teeth.

"Besides, I don't think it would be a very good day to run off with someone," I say. "Doesn't your husband have to preach tomorrow—I mean, today?"

Mrs. Lawson looks at me like I'm the devil.

I remember the note Mama left and figure that it must still be near the eyes and fingers of the wronged wife. One of the first things I need to do is get that away from her.

I walk over and take the folded sheet off the counter. I look at it, then say, "No, this isn't it; this is my grocery list for next week." I'm calm and sound, I think, quite believable.

I yawn. "It must be in the back," I add.

I walk back to my bedroom and shuffle things noisily as if I'm looking for something, then come back empty-handed, shrugging my shoulders. "I haven't been able to remember things real well since I hit my head," I say, slowly sitting back down on the sofa.

"That's right!" Aunt Doris says definsive-like. "This child has just come through a major trauma. She doesn't need us to bother her at this ungodly hour."

She turns to the preacher's wife as if Mrs. Lawson had just disturbed the intensive-care unit. "You want her relapse on your conscience?" Then she walks to the door, opens it, and flings her still-glowing cigarette onto the driveway.

Grandma moves next to me and pulls back my bangs to show the aging bruise as proof of my having no knowledge of Mama's whereabouts.

Mrs. Lawson appears to be coming unraveled. "I know that you Ivy women are lying. And you're protecting that slut sister of yours." She says this to Doris, who looks like she's going to rear back and hit her.

"You poisoned hussies think you know so much, think you're better than everybody else," the preacher's wife screeches. "Well, I'm going to find the two of them; and when I do, there will be hell to pay!" She backs out repeating herself: "Hell to pay!"

Doris holds open the door while Mrs. Lawson backs past her. "Yeah, well, being married to a preacher, you should know all about that," she snaps. "Why don't you check out the cemetery. Maybe he's trying to revive some of those he bored to death!"

Mrs. Lawson stalks to her car without further comment and drives away. Doris walks back in and shuts the door.

"Now that's a sick woman," she says. She sits down in the chair next to the sofa. "Anybody that hard up for a man that she'd go waking people up from a cold sleep!"

"Seems like I remember a time or two you've gone searching for some misguided husband yourself," Grandma says, leaning back in her seat.

"Yeah, but at least it won't no preacher." Then she looks to me. "Now tell us about this dream."

I take a deep breath and think back. I remember that many of the images spoke clearly of Cordessa and Sterling and their imminent reunion. I don't, however, understand why Mama was in the same cloud. But I realize that instead of discussing this, I need to get to the creek and warn Mama about Mrs. Lawson.

"It was a storm," I say, trying to appease her. "And everybody had the life sucked out of them."

Doris nods like she's thinking; and Grandma understands the reading of my voice and the fact that I know where Mama is. "Come on, Doris. Tessa needs her sleep."

I get up first and help Grandma off the couch.

"We'll leave you the car and we'll walk back," Grandma says.

"Walk back?" Aunt Doris asks, surprised. "At five in the morning?"

"We'll be fine," Grandma replies. "The moon is bright, and I could use the exercise." Then she winks at Doris, who seems to realize that I'm going to find Mama.

"Why doesn't Tessa just drop us off on her way out?" she suggests.

I love the way our family talks, in half-sentences, but all defined.

"I can do that," I say. "Let me go put on some clothes."

We meet outside and then all get in the car. Grandma sits up front as I put the key in the ignition.

"This storm in your dream," Aunt Doris says, looking like a child with a brand-new penny as she leans against the front seat from the back, "was there an eye?"

Instantly a cold chill moves up and down my back like the steel blade of a knife. I look at her in the rearview mirror, and she stares back like there's something she already Knows. I shake my head no, unwilling to talk about the dream now, and drop them off with a sense of relief.

When I get on the path to Sandy Creek, I turn off my lights so I won't scare them when I drive up. And as I get closer to the makeshift cabin I can tell that somebody's inside. Looking around, I notice the same car I saw hours earlier. It was pulled so far off the path, almost hidden by trees, that I hadn't seen it when Sterling and I were up by the creek.

I park some hundred yards away, thinking that maybe I can quietly tap on the door and let Mama know that it's me. Even though there's a light coming from the shack, I assume that they're both asleep at this early hour.

I left my flashlight at home, so I walk in darkness, trying not to move off the path and into the grass that I remember grows long and tangled on both sides.

When I get to the side of the cabin, I can see my mother's face through a small, dusty window. She's awake, talking. I can hear her voice, tearful like she's confessing as she speaks to the man before her, who I can only assume is the preacher. They're fully clothed, which makes me feel better; and a candle, a bottle of something, and an open book—a Bible, I guess—are situated between them.

"This isn't your doing, Bertie," the preacher says quietly, almost like he's praying.

Curious but afraid, I decide to wait before interrupting.

"The Lord knows you made the only decision you knew how," the preacher says.

Mama is crying full-out now, and I'm afraid to walk in.

"You've made your confession; you've been anointed; and now you've got to let go of the past."

"I can't," my mama says in a torrent of tears. "Because that boy is here; and just to see his face again can only remind me of everything evil I know."

There's a pause as she wipes her eyes.

"Bertie, we've been through this," he chides gently.

I can tell that the preacher is wanting to leave. And I'm surprised that this looks more like a church meeting than some sexual rendezvous. He sticks his hands in his pockets, then pulls them out and looks at his wristwatch.

Just then I see a shadow on the opposite wall and realize that the two of them aren't alone.

"Sweet Bertie," the other voice says, "just because something began in evil doesn't mean it's got to end up that way."

I strain to make out the voice.

"Lord yes, Bertie," Reverend Lawson says, closing the book.

Suddenly I hear the other voice start to hum, and I recognize now that it's Reverend Renfrow there on the other side of the small room; and I Know that he Knows I'm here. I freeze for a minute, not sure what I should do. I slowly walk back to the car and watch as the candle goes out in the cabin. Then I start the engine and head down the path until I'm on the lake road and can turn on my lights and push hard on the gas pedal.

I sit at the intersection of the lake road with the main road for what seems like a long time trying to figure things out—the premonitions, the meeting of Mama with the preachers there at the mouth of Sandy Creek, her recollection of evil, mothers and their children, and the dream of a violent cloud.

I wonder what to do next. I think about going home or driving over to the Airstream to see if Sterling is back or going to the bar to find out if he's gone to talk to Cordessa. I think about waking up Liddy and getting her to ride along with me or asking Grandma and Doris what would be best.

Then out of nowhere or everywhere I get a strange and unusual notion that seems to pull and blend everything together like the little folded bag that holds in the leaves of tea. The idea boils and steeps, and I sit up and jerk the little string on top. Then I drive hard and straight to the other side of town.

With the sun slowly rising on a midsummer Sunday in Pleasant Cross, I'm flying dead-center, headlong, and Knowing into the eye of the storm.

6

The Belly of Truth

🌿 By the time I've gotten to the clean side of town, the sun has climbed above the street signs and the tops of trees. The air is already damp and thick, the sky heavy and close. Birds are alert and busy, squirrels nervously gathering the day's meals. The only other car I see on the streets is that of Mr. Hodges, who's delivering the Sunday paper.

I creep along the roads, up Maple, then right on Elm, where the willows form a canopy from side to side. Left on Main and then straight down through the magazine houses—the ones that could have come out of *Southern Life*—until I park right in front of the big house at the end.

Lynne Hinton

Mr. Hodges pulls up behind my car, looks curiously at me, then tosses the paper so that it lands on the driveway, dead-center of the garage door. I wave, real friendly-like, as if I'm waiting for someone to come out and join me. He just turns his head and goes to the next street over.

I sit here in my car, on this early July morning, on a street that I've never driven or played on, in front of a house that I'd never be invited to, and wonder about this kind of life that I've never known.

I look at the neatly manicured lawn, the strong and regal peonies, wide like the mouths of frogs, and the brilliant, well-watered geraniums that line the walkway. I recognize the stacked auburn pine needles that circle around azaleas and rhododendrons and the pink and white dogwoods, all tight and bunched without a single piece loose or straying.

I see the hidden sprinklers in the lush green grass and the small marble rabbits, two of them, evenly spaced and facing each other, sitting on the opposite sides of the first step to the front porch.

❧

I notice the shine in the windows, the fresh paint along the sills, and the evenness in the lay of the smooth pink bricks. The gutters are empty, and the roof looks new and washed. Everything outside is neat and penned, kept in its place.

It's not a huge house; there are larger ones, in fact, across the street. But this one is long and sturdy, well thought-through and planned. No piercing wind or menacing cloud will ever take *this* one down. It's a fortress of pride, a man's only castle and a woman's crowning jewel. It sits like a palace that everyone else has built their homes around. It's the ending of the street or the beginning of the town, depending upon which way you're standing.

I know that inside this house are glossy hardwood floors, stark white walls, and charming paintings of old Charleston plantations mixed with oil portraits of well-mannered children. The furniture, unblemished and polished in lemon oil, was all hand-picked and delivered by an interior designer from Charlotte or Raleigh.

The bathroom has a deep claw-footed tub

with porcelain fixtures that lend the room an antique feeling. The towels are plush cotton the color of dusty rose. The beds are downy and soft; and except for the hard kingsize pillow that's used in the master bedroom, all of the cushions are goosedown and light.

There's a pleasant smell inside, I can already tell—an easy, perfumed scent that makes you look around to try to find its source. Large three-wicked candles and fresh garden flowers fill every room, so that to visit here would almost make you think you were a guest in some country inn.

That's the way Mrs. Jenkins would want her house to feel—like a welcome place, an honorable place, an inviting and tidy place. But a house like this is good only for brief, arranged visits.

Grandchildren are loved but always held, never left alone at any time. Men are permitted to sit down and rest in the creamy oversized sofa but are frowned upon if they widen their legs or drape an arm too carelessly along the top. Ladies are expected to be comfortable in the kitchen but are quickly escorted out if they rest too lazily against the countertop or take a cookie from the platter before being served.

This degree of household order and display requires firm, deliberate rules. And though they're not announced in the beginning, as they are when you first check into a motel, after a few mistakes and a couple of lengthy, glowering looks you know what they are. And if you can't follow them, your stay is cut short so that the household can be kept intact.

I sit out front and wait for more than an hour, thinking these kinds of thoughts, then twist my neck to watch as a light goes on and curtains are separated in the window of an upstairs room. In a few seconds the garage door opens and Mr. Jenkins, in his boxer shorts and an open robe, comes out to get the morning paper. He looks up as I get out of the car, his eyes squinting and small.

"Tyrus Jenkins," I say.

He watches me without saying a word, his eyebrows knitted in a cluster of wrinkles and his mouth twisted in a bend.

"You know who I am?" I ask, moving to stand right in front of him. I'm wearing jeans and a shirt that says BIG DOGS RUN WHERE THEY WANT.

He stares then shakes his head no in a slow and teasing way.

"I'm Tessa Ivy," I say, thinking that the name will mean something to him.

"Bertie's daughter," I add, like that should do it.

He raises his eyebrows now and lowers the paper, but he still doesn't say anything. Then his wife opens the back door, the one that goes into the garage, and sees us standing there.

"Who's that, Tyrus?" she asks, trying to sound friendly. "If that's Howard, tell him I don't want him working on the pool today. The bridge club is coming over." She sticks her head out more and tries to identify my shape against the sun. "Is that Howard?"

"No," her husband shouts without turning around. "Just go on back in."

"Oh," she whispers, like she's been stung by a yellow jacket. Then the door closes.

"You lost or run out of gas?" He glances over

to the car, then clears his throat and sticks one hand in the pocket of his robe.

I see Mrs. Jenkins peeking through the front window now. He sees me watching her and glares in her direction. She turns and walks out of the room.

"You do know my mama, don't you?" I'm close enough to see him thinking.

"Her and Cordessa Pender. Gordon then, I believe," I say, remembering what Reverend Renfrow called her. "You knew them both, didn't you?"

He cuts his eyes away from me and glances over the top of my head. A neighbor has come out and is staring in our direction. Mr. Jenkins raises his chin, acknowledging him.

"That was my brother, Donald," he says, still looking toward the neighbor. "He was the one who got tied up with that gal and your mama." Then he opens up the paper like maybe he's through.

"What do you mean, 'tied up'?" I ask, stepping even closer.

He folds back up the paper and looks down at

me. It's a cold, searching fix. Then he starts to laugh like he's seen something he hadn't noticed before.

"You come busting up here first thing on a Sunday morning like you're going to accuse me of something," he says with a sneer, "and you poor white Ivy trash don't know anything." Then he turns to walk inside.

I march right behind and then step in front of him. We're just inside the garage.

"I know that you're a dirty son of a bitch and that you did something to Cordessa Gordon."

"Yeah, I did something all right. I gave her the loan so that she could buy that cheap redneck bar," he says, like he's clean.

I take a step back.

"And I let your mammy keep that old broken-down farmhouse." He pushes me aside and walks toward the steps leading from the garage into the house, then turns to add, "I didn't *have* to do anything for either one of them."

He hits the automatic button to close the garage door, and I step outside quickly so as not to be locked in. The door brushes against my arm as it glides down.

I stand unmoving for a minute or so. When I look up, I see Mrs. Jenkins peeking at me again through the window. Half-hidden by the pulled-away curtain, she looks disheveled and confused, and she's chewing on her bottom lip. It looks like she's locked in there, like a child sent to her room. I hear Mr. Jenkins yell, and the curtain falls back in place.

After I realize that he isn't coming back out and that I have no real reason to go back in, I get in the car and drive away. The traffic has picked up since I arrived. Because it's a holiday weekend, people are out and about, driving to the mountains or the beach or on their way back home.

When I get to Cordessa's place, Sterling's truck is parked on the side, and I wonder if he's been here all night or if he drove around awhile before coming to see her. I pull up; but I keep the car running, still trying to decide if maybe I shouldn't let them have more time to learn each other. I figure that by now, though, they've heard the engine and know that somebody's out front. So I turn off the car, get out, and knock on the door.

Cordessa answers it. I can tell at first that she thinks I'm Liddy; then, because my hair is natural brown and Liddy has a new shade for the summer, she turns around to the inside and yells out, "It's for you." Then she leaves the door open and shuffles to the back.

It's dark in the bar, musty and still smoky from last night. Sterling is sitting at a table, drinking a can of Budweiser. He looks tired, stringy. Cordessa sits back down across from him, where she's been for awhile, I guess. And she kicks out a chair beside her, inviting me to join them. I close the door.

She lights up a cigarette. "Seems the two of you already know each other," she says, breaking up the hush.

Sterling nods and smiles up at me.

I sit down.

"Get you something to drink?" Cordessa asks.

"Mountain Dew," Sterling says, getting up to find me one.

He goes around the bar and looks behind the counter.

"You'll have to fish one out of the cooler in the kitchen," Cordessa says.

He comes out from behind the bar and goes through the back door.

She inspects me like she's trying to read my mind. "You out awful early."

"Yes, ma'am," I say.

"Girl, don't be saying *yes ma'am* to me. I ain't that old." She sits up straighter when she says this.

She looks at me real hard, then turns towards the kitchen, where we hear Sterling trying to find me a soda.

"You know everything, I guess," she says, facing away like she's ashamed.

"No, ma'am," I reply, trying to be respectful, then remembering that she told me not say *ma'am*. "Not *everything*."

When she shifts herself back around, I look at

her face. It's silky and brown as chocolate. There are a few lines around her mouth and at the corners of her eyes, but mostly she seems young and unbruised.

"You and Liddy favor your mama," she says. She's been watching me too. She takes a hit off her cigarette, then rolls the tip of it around in the ashtray, which is full of butts.

"I guess so," I reply.

"I told your sister she shouldn't come to work here, but she wouldn't listen." Cordessa slides back in her chair.

"She doesn't much," I answer. "Listen, I mean," I add.

We hear Sterling banging around.

"Is he all right?" I ask, like I have the right to know.

She nods affirmatively. "Better than I would've thought if I was told he was coming."

She draws a steady drag, swallows a bit, then blows out the rest.

"You know about me and your mama?" she asks, holding her hands still like it takes some effort and staring at me real deep in the eyes.

❦

I glance away. "Some," I say. Then, for reasons I don't know, I add, "I just came from Mr. Jenkins."

Her hand comes up to her mouth and she starts to say something, but just then Sterling comes back in the room.

"Can only find a Mello Yello. Hope that'll do." He shoves the door shut with the bottom of his foot and walks over to the table. He opens the can and sets it down before me.

"Thanks," I say, lifting it to drink. It's sweet and warm, some of it rolling down my chin.

Cordessa hands me a napkin from her pocket, and I wipe off the lower part of my face.

I ask her about the cookout, which she says was a huge success except the fireworks, which fizzled and had very little pop. Then we're quiet again, and I look over to Sterling.

I see his mother in him now as he sits across from us: her shoulders pushing up against a weight that nobody names; her quick, shifty glances that follow movement and recognize footsteps; a grave sense of preparedness that was cast upon them both by somebody else's doing; and a distant cleaving to that which is slow and easy.

"How did you find out about me?" Cordessa asks after taking a swallow of her own drink— something in a tall, skinny glass with melting ice.

"Saw a picture," I answer, "in their trailer. Then I recognized you last evening at the cookout."

"Yeah?" she asks, a little cheerful. "I still look the same?" She elbows me to show that she's joking.

I shrug and look over to Sterling, who isn't saying anything except to ask if my soda is okay. He must be a little drunk. He seems kind of sloppy in a way I haven't seen him before.

Cordessa fills me in on some of the story she's obviously already told Sterling. "I heard about Reverend Renfrow from my Aunt Mozelle. She said that he was a real decent man and seemed lonesome for a son."

A piece of hair has fallen down her forehead. She pulls it between her fingers, studies it like she's trying to understand why it came down.

Then she brushes it back and sticks it under the flat part on top.

"Seems like he did all right by you," she says to her son, half-questioning.

Sterling nods and sucks his teeth. He still isn't saying anything. He reaches across the table and takes my hand, in affection I think.

Cordessa raises an eyebrow.

"Your mama know about this?" she says, looking at our hands.

I nod.

"She know what you know?" She's peering at me dead-aim, straight in the eyes now. "That Sterling's my son?"

"I'm not sure," I reply. "She knows *something*, though."

Cordessa lets out a deep breath, crushes her cigarette in the ashtray, stands, and starts to clean up around us.

Sterling rests his head on the arm that's reaching out to me. He looks in my face, smiles with only the tiniest hint of sorrow, then closes his eyes, like he's falling asleep.

"You always think when you're young that your friends will be there forever," Cordessa says, wiping off a chair. "Least *I* did," she adds.

I let go of Sterling's hand, but he doesn't seem to notice. He's passed out or asleep or both. I get up to help Cordessa clean.

"But that's the funny thing about trouble," she says, putting all the glasses on one tabletop, the cans and bottles on another. "You assume it will automatically keep people together, especially old friends. But it ain't always so." She goes behind the bar to get a rack and a trash can. "Ain't always so," she repeats.

I pick up a bottle from under a nearby table and stand there, just holding it in my hands.

"Did you know that the divorce rate is higher in families with sick kids than in those with healthy ones?" she asks, resting the plastic rack on her hip.

"Seems odd, don't it? I mean, you'd think with a sick child the mama and the daddy would be closer than usual—you know, be drawn to each other because of what they come through. But," she says, twisting her mouth in a funny way, "it don't work that way." She sets the rack down.

"Something about torment or crisis just hangs on people like an old coat. So that when you get through it, looks like that other person can only remind you of the bad things. Gets to be like feeling haunted, I guess. And after awhile, you just want to be free of it, so you fall away."

She starts to place empty glasses in the rack to be washed, and I follow her example. We clean for awhile without talking.

Finally I ask, "You and Mama get in trouble with one of the Jenkinses?" I go over and put trash in the container she brought out earlier, then move away to give her space for the truth.

She braces herself on the rack and leans forward, toward Sterling. "We've been up since midnight," Cordessa says, nodding at the sleeping figure. Her face softens and she turns to blink away tears. "Pretty much told him everything."

"Guess he's tired," I say, glancing over at him.

She pushes back her hair and then starts to empty ashtrays. I collect more glasses and take them over to where she's standing.

"We were just girls," she says, answering the question about the Jenkinses, I suppose. She stacks the ashtrays, then places the glasses upside down in the rack. "Younger than you and Liddy," she continues.

I put the bottles in the recycling can next to the bar, trying not to make too much noise.

"Your mama had a big crush on Donald, and she was in way over her head," Cordessa says, heading to a closet to get a towel. "There was some party she heard about, and we went together. It was the late seventies," she says, like I'd understand what that timeframe meant.

"Neither one of us had any business being on that side of town, but your mama," Cordessa says, shaking her head and blowing out smoke from a new cigarette, "she was determined to get near Donald Jenkins."

Sterling shifts a little in his seat, and Cordessa stops, like maybe she doesn't want him to hear details about names and dates. When he goes quiet again, she starts back telling the story, now in a softer voice.

"Anyway, it was a setup, won't no party. And

your mama and me ended up in a house with Donald Jenkins and a bunch of other mean, drunk, white college boys." Now the story falls out, fast and all over, like rain.

"Some of them took her off to another room, and I heard her screaming. But there wasn't anything I could do, 'cause a couple of 'em were all on top of me by then." Cordessa takes in a deep breath, a long drag.

There's a pause now, as weighted as quarry rock, the shower having passed.

"Tyrus drove us home, dropped us off at the lake drive." She lets out the first part of a laugh. "He almost seemed sorry for us." Then she thinks a moment.

"I guess later he suffered from a bad case of the guilts, because he approved me a loan ten years ago when I didn't have no business getting money." She glances around the bar like she's thinking how it used to be.

"And I expect you and your grandma's houses are still standing for the same reason."

I think about what he told me earlier.

"Everybody said he actually owns all the

land," she says, fitting one more glass in the last row of the rack.

"Guess he thought he was making up for his family's evil. But it'd take more than an old bar and a couple of family homes to redeem that lot of meanness." She looks down at her hands.

"Anyway, about me and your mama—after it happened, we didn't say nothing to each other." Cordessa picks up the rack of dirty glassware.

"It was like it busted us up somehow inside; and instead of binding us together, like you'd think such a thing would do," she turns her clear eyes to mine, "it just pulled everything apart."

She carries the rack into the kitchen, turns on the dishwasher, and after some time walks back in.

I pick up chairs and turn them upside down on the tables. I'm trying to stay focused on cleaning, but then a question rises too close to the surface not to ask.

"Mama get pregnant too?" The words feel all cracked and broken, like I do inside.

Cordessa nods and turns towards the small

bit of light coming through the front-door window. "She went to Goldston, to the clinic." She pauses. "I don't reckon anybody ever knew."

Then she puts out her cigarette, gets a broom from the closet, and starts to sweep.

And I think, So that's it, then. That's the reason for the dark and cloudy dream and the leaves in my tea and the longing in my mother's heart to be forgiven or relieved. That's the reason she can't be near Cordessa, and that's why Liddy can't find Renfrow in my palm. It's a *J* that's there, for Jenkins or Jones or James or some other last name from a boy who forced himself upon a naive teenaged girl and left his seed for evil.

Evil, I think. But then I look over at Sterling. And I don't see any evil in him. I see only gentleness and purity, like the unsoiled manner of his name. Maybe Mama thinks he represents something that rips and tears open the dreams of young women, but I know better. I know that this boy set in honey is a part of everything good I'll ever regard again.

I try to untangle all these things in my mind as

Cordessa sweeps the trash into a dustpan and goes into the kitchen to dump it out.

She comes back, and as we quietly clean the tables and floors, trying not to awaken the sleeping boy who connects us, we look at each other differently. We seem to be aware that we're now forever bound because of him, and more—the story and the memories and an old friendship and these new ones, and all of the badness and the goodness in Knowing the truth.

Cordessa seems satisfied in a way I didn't see her to be yesterday; and even though Sterling now has to sort through fears and ideas he'd thought were locked away, I have the queerest notion that everything is going to be okay. Then, just as I'm starting to consider the positive possibilities, there's a knock at the door.

Sterling sits up and wipes his brown eyes. Cordessa walks over and swings the door open. Mama and Liddy walk in looking like bad news is all over them.

"Hey, C," my mama says slow, like she's just remembering how it feels to say such a thing.

"Bertie," Cordessa replies, not cold or uncaring, just a little further away than she is.

They stand like this on opposite sides of the door until Liddy finally pushes through and comes over to me. She pulls me near the far side of the bar where Sterling can't hear.

"Reverend Renfrow's had a stroke," she says.

I glance over to Mama, who shakes her head no, leading me to the conclusion that he isn't likely to make it. Then I turn towards Sterling, who's getting up from the table and throwing his cans in the recycling bin. He looks at Cordessa and Mama, then at me and Liddy.

"What's wrong?" he asks, innocent but weary.

There's a pause as we all look at each other, wondering who's going to tell him what happened.

"It's your father," Cordessa finally says. "Reverend Renfrow."

I walk over and put my hand on his arm.

He looks around at each one of us again.

"He's at the hospital," Mama explains. "He's had a stroke."

I take Sterling by the hand. We walk past everybody and go out to his truck. Then I get the keys and drive us to the hospital. He stares out the window the whole way, not saying a thing.

When we get there, Reverend Lawson is in the waiting room. He stands up and comes over to Sterling and me. "It's pretty bad, young man," he says, like he's practiced. "We found him at the lake, right before church."

I look at the clock on the wall and realize that Reverend Lawson is missing Sunday services. Mama must have started Knowing after they left the creek and then chased the preacher back up to the church to ask for help.

It isn't long before a doctor walks in and looks around the room. He searches the preacher's face, then they both turn to Sterling.

"I'm Dr. Trudeau," he says. He's chubby in his white coat, an ID badge on the pocket, and his arms hang uselessly from the elbow-length sleeves.

"I was here when they brought your father in," he says. I suspect he's trying to be sympathetic, but he comes off sounding like a teacher.

❦

"There was a massive hemorrhage in the brain." He shakes his balding head and looks away. "I'm afraid your daddy didn't make it." The doctor folds his arms across his chest and nods up and down like a doll with a spring in its neck.

Me and Sterling sit down together. I close my eyes and start to feel an old and distant pull in my chest. I hold tightly to Sterling's hand. It feels cold and limp.

"We've got him in a room, if you'd like to go and see him." The doctor has his hand on the doorknob. You can tell that he's eager to leave.

Both Reverend Lawson and I stand up at the same time, in a gesture that we'll go with him. But Sterling just shakes his head no. He doesn't want to go.

"Okay," the doctor says. There's a pause. "Do you know anything about the arrangements you'll make?"

Sterling looks at me. I shrug my shoulders, unsure what he's asking.

"A funeral home?" the doctor prompts.

"Lynch's." Mama and Liddy and Cordessa

have come in behind the doctor, and Mama takes over. "Lynch's Funeral Home on South Main." She sounds so professional. "We'll take care of everything."

The doctor nods and gives a formal smile. "The nurse will be right in to take down the information," he says. "After that, you're free to go." Then he hurries out the door.

Everybody sits down. For several minutes we're lost in our own thoughts. A television blares a gospel music show the whole time, and I keep noticing Reverend Lawson looking up to see it.

"Your daddy sure loved you," Cordessa says finally, like she knows more than the rest of us.

Sterling just nods.

"Will you want to take him back to Nevada?" my mother asks. She's curious, I guess, about what's going to happen.

He shakes his head.

We sit in this awkwardness for awhile, and then Preacher Lawson says, "Oh, I have something for you, Sterling—a letter that your dad wrote and gave to me a couple of days ago."

He fiddles in his pocket and pulls out an envelope with Sterling's name on it. "He came to the church and said I'd need to give it to you sometime."

Liddy and Mama and me glance around at each other. We understand that Reverend Renfrow had a Knowing all his own.

Sterling takes the envelope and holds it in his hands for a long time, just looking at his name, the letters, the edges, front and back.

As he turns it upside down, a stone and a flower petal fall out, landing between my feet. The rock is a small chip of turquoise, the bluest stone I've ever seen. I pick it up and roll it around in my fingers. It's like the deepest part of the lake, the center where it's coldest and fair, the place where I've never touched the bottom. It's like the wide break of sky that dares any cloud to pass across it, a blue so clean and unsullied that it reminds me of innocence.

The petal is from a tiger lily, bright orange and soft as velvet. I rub it across my cheek; then I hold the two colors in my hands so that Sterling can see them, the lake and the sun, the union of two colors from a dream that belong together, two colors that are now understood. But he doesn't seem to care.

The letter, he says, he wants to read by himself.

And so we all get up to walk out. And everybody touches him, on the head, across the cheek, along his back, and on his neck. But we leave him there, me included. I put his keys on the empty chair beside him, kneel down in front of him, thinking I'll have something to say when I get real close. But I don't. So I just lay my head in his lap, placing the turquoise and the flower on his leg just above the knee.

After I get up and go a little ways, I turn around to look at him. He's just sitting there with his face down, his fingers running along the edges of the envelope, the blessing from his father balanced on his thigh. I want to run to him and hold him, find a way to make everything all right, but Liddy comes up beside me and walks with me out the door.

7

The Wide and Pleasant Road

It's been a rainy summer for North Carolina. Usually by this time in July the earth is brittle, brown, and cracked. But this year things are still green and fresh and growing.

It's the best garden I've had since five years or more. No spider mites or bottom rot or scales have crowded out any of the plants. There's been no need for a second dousing of fertilizer or an extra bag of lime. The corn is waist-high, the tomatoes are starting to produce crimson fruit, and the cucumbers and squash lay like crooked green and yellow fingers all along the rows.

Though it's been a summer of truth and death, and the peeling away of a story, it will stand out in my memories as a season of sharp and rapid growth.

Reverend Lawson held a brief service out at the lake the Tuesday after Sterling's daddy died. Me and Mama, Liddy, Grandma, Doris, and Cordessa stood around Sterling dropping rose petals at the bank as the dead man's ashes were spilled all around us.

Reverend Renfrow flew in the air as small pieces of soot, a silky dust, then floated back in our faces, on our clothes, and gathered in the beads of sweat down along our necks.

We sang "Trouble in My Way," which Cordessa led and we followed, since none of us knew how to sing an old spiritual. She sang it like she knew it, all her life, every day. Sterling knew it too, but he didn't really make any noise; he just moved his lips along with us.

After the song there was a reading from Psalms—"The Lord Is My Shepherd"—and a prayer; and then Sterling surprised everyone,

since he'd been so quiet, and read the last letter
Reverend Renfrow had written.

It went like this:

Dear Boy,

*I imagine you're hot with me right now, bring-
ing you to such a place as this and then leaving
you. The Lord came to me back in Rowland and
told me that I didn't have much time. And I
knew then and there that it was only right that
you come home to your mama.*

*I never knew there to be such a thing as a
Pleasant Cross; but I expect if I had to stick a label on you, it would be just that. I raised you
from a baby because your mama couldn't keep
you and I hated to see a black child growing up
in the arms of the state. Since I was the first one
she contacted, I followed her offer like a sign
from God and took you up like a cross to bear.
But you been like the treasure hidden in the
field, pure sweetness for me, ever since.*

Now I figure you'll hear some hard stories

about where you came from and how you got
here, but none of that stuff matters. You're here
now; and you're the breath of life and marked
with holy.

All I have is in that trailer. It's yours now,
that and the old truck. Keep the filters changed
and watch out for the hoses. Remember never to
take more than you need. Don't drive when
you're angry. Always bless God for the bounty
of goodness. And fish on the north side of a lake
in the morning, the south side in the evening.

In closing then, Boy, you know all you need
to know. I figure I taught you the best I had, and
that's always been aplenty for me. Don't be
afraid if the Lord still comes around and visits. I
reckon he'll be a little lonesome without ol'
Moses around to chew the fat, and I think he's
sort of partial to the Airstream.

I love you, Boy—always have.

The Reverend Moses T. Renfrow

Sterling read the letter strong and real proud.
Then he folded it back up and stuck it in the

pocket on the left side of his shirt. Then he took me by the hand and we all stood quiet in this small gathering of sorrow and celebration.

It was early—ten or so in the morning—when we finished. Just as we turned to go, two geese, brown with black wings, soared above our heads and dropped in the center of the lake. We watched them for awhile, dipping and gliding and hoisting themselves gracefully in that sheer patch of sapphire.

Then we all went back to the house for Mama's pork and Liddy's biscuits. About eleven-thirty Grandma called for rain, and the preacher and Doris walked out touching hands and looking real suspicious. Grandma snorted through her nose like she Knew it was time for trouble. And Mama just shook her head and laughed. Liddy painted Cordessa's nails while Sterling and I walked through the garden, past the pine trees, and out to the middle of the brown and golden meadow. I lay down, looking upwards, waiting for the sky to break open.

While I lay there, he slipped in beside me like the dolphin in my dream; and when I stared up at the sky, I felt myself finally pushing all the way through to the surface of blueness and then higher, until I was straightened out and carried on the wind to the strong orange sun, my dream and my life in careful balance. Within minutes an easy shower fell about us. We stayed together outside, there in an afternoon storm on the day of his father's funeral, tangled and tied in tenderness and not giving in to the sadness.

Today, four days later, I've packed up my sister's four suitcases and taken them to the bus station as I stand in the passing of the final leaf of tea.

Liddy met Mr. Lynch's nephew from Georgia, Thomas Orville; and she's head-over-heels fallen for this boy, who's already had two years of community college. He's here in Pleasant Cross because he's learning to be a funeral director. Mama figures he's next in line for the family business.

My sister ran into him when we were making arrangements for Reverend Renfrow's cremation and service. This was Thomas's first experience with a burning of the body, and his hands shook and his neck got all red when Mr. Lynch explained to everybody how it was to be done.

Liddy found that sort of reaction tender and felt right away that he was more than just the love in her hand: he was the right choice. So she hooked onto him with eyes and heart, and that college boy doesn't stand a chance.

It isn't Liddy, though, who's going to Atlanta. It's me. Thomas Orville is staying in Pleasant Cross for good, so my sister seems to have done away with her wanderlust. She's learning to fix hair and makeup on dead people, waiting for Thomas to understand what's already come to pass.

She's gone to work at Lynch's with Mama, and I don't know how they'll survive each other working and living together. But I guess they'll find a way.

Sterling took the Airstream up to the mountains in Asheville, then over to South Carolina, where Reverend Renfrow had family. He thought it was only right to tell them in person and let them walk in his daddy's trailer and remember him from the last place he stood.

We decided it would be fun to meet in Atlanta and then travel down along the southern states, see a little of the country and spend some good, long time together.

Mama and Grandma have said that we ought to have a summer wedding, out by the lake, then a party at Cordessa's bar. And the way things are turning out, I figure that could very well be a part of my future.

I don't look too much, though, to Knowing about tomorrow. After all, I'm on a bus, ready to head for places I've never seen, to join up with a man to whom I only just gave away my heart. It seems I've got enough on my hands sorting through today and trying to make sense of yesterday. I don't really think I want to learn more than what I already know.

It's like I remember Grandma saying when I was just a little girl, "A body could know everything there is to know about the future, but that don't guarantee happiness."

Then I recall how she threw a blade of grass in the air and watched it twirl and fall. Reading the spinning grass, she said, "Storm's coming; better cover our heads." And she walked inside.

I see her now, her and Mama, Liddy and Doris, standing there by the bus garage, holding hands, waving and weeping, like things are different now that I'm leaving. And I guess they are. Growing up changes you and everybody you love.

Liddy says it's made us smarter, but I think it's just made me notice things more.

I've noticed, for instance, that most folks hurry through life, looking for some edge in knowing the future, hoping to secure for themselves a tiny piece of contentment by getting a jump on everybody else. Only to discover, usually much too late, that the most wonderful things are the things they already have right at their feet, the things they got when they were little-bitty, the things they keep in their hearts.

And I've noticed that all through your life, whether you know it or not, you collect stuff, remember things. Hard things like the eyes of the people who hurt you, the chill in the wake of evil; smooth things like the color in your mind when a good dream comes true or a brown-sugar boy who hands you a piece of the sun; and kind things like the smiles and the hands and the memories of the ones who love you most. You let go and you hold on. And sometimes it's like you're not even sure which you've done.

Even if you have a Knowing, an extra sense of reading the future, it's these scraps of yesterday that coat and cover everything of today and wind up shaping your tomorrow. It's these slices of life that always end up being the things you Know best.

I wave good-bye to the huddled women, wipe a few tears from my eyes, and turn around in my seat to look out the big front window.

The bus pulls away from the station, and I hear somebody—the old lady sitting behind me, I think—say, "My, what a wide and pleasant road."

I see the tall, strong trees bending in the breeze, the painted horizon of a rich summer sky, the rocks in the asphalt that shine like jewels; and I say, "Amen."

Welcome back to Hope Springs!

The small North Carolina town comes alive again in *Garden of Faith*, the sequel to Lynne Hinton's bestselling and acclaimed first novel *Friendship Cake*. The ladies of Hope Springs Church have finished the cookbook that brought them together, and now their bonds of friendship are put to the test when they are faced with major life changes and decisions. Interspersed throughout are Bea's Botanical Bits—unforgettable snippets of advice that help to cultivate the garden, as well as the spirit.

Praise for *Garden of Faith*

"... an anthem to friendship ... To miss it
is to deny yourself a small treasure."
Jacquelyn Mitchard, author of *The Deep End of the Ocean*

"In *Garden of Faith* a beautiful story grows side by side
with powerful truth. It caused my soul to bloom."
Philip Gulley, author of *Front Porch Tales*
and *Home to Harmony*

Garden of Faith will be available in hardcover
from HarperCollins May 2002

Hope Springs
Community Garden Club
Newsletter Volume 1, Number 3

Bea's Botanical Bits

A Dirty Subject

Girls, let's talk dirty. Have you checked the soil in your garden lately? Are your tomatoes getting dry rot, or are your pepper plants not as sturdy as last year? Then maybe you need to put a few strips of newspaper around the roots or buy a little fertilizer. Check the nitrogen level and add a bit of lime.

Soil content affects the nature of your produce. My cousin, who lives near the coast, swears that watermelon is sweeter there because the sandy soil is more sugary than our claylike dirt here. But I wouldn't know about that.

You can always spice up your dirt with what is delicately referred to as "cow tea." I'm talking manure, sisters. And don't act offended. You know a little dung goes a long way.

Good soil is the most important key to growing a bountiful and healthy garden.

✿ "As the president of the Women' Guild . . ." Beatrice wanted to get the meeting started so that she could show her honeymoon pictures.

"Beatrice Newgarden Witherspoon, if you don't shut up with that call to order, I'm going to announce to the church that you had sex before you got married." Louise pushed her way onto the sofa and flopped down next to Jessie.

Charlotte laughed.

Beatrice rolled her eyes and opened up the box that carried her pictures. She began sorting the small albums so that she could keep the trip in photographic sequence.

Even though the cookbook had been com

pleted months ago, the committee continued to meet. Working on the cookbook, Beatrice had discovered that she enjoyed writing. And since she had always loved to garden, the Garden Club newsletter seemed like the next perfect project. But she couldn't seem to say good-bye to the women from the committee.

Beatrice kept calling her friends together even after the cookbook manuscript was finished and sent to the printer. She manufactured reasons why they had to meet until finally Jessie recognized what she was doing and suggested that they simply come together once a month, just to talk, stay connected. It was a welcomed idea, and Beatrice was only too glad not to have to make up reasons to call everyone.

They met at each woman's house, rotating the schedule. The hostess was in charge of refreshments, though they didn't expect or desire anything too elaborate. Tonight they were at Jessie's. She had some leftover pound cake and a few strawberries, coffee and lemonade. It was quiet in the house since Lana and Wallace had gone out to dinner, the baby was sleeping, and

James Senior was out back working on his car. Everyone had arrived, and Beatrice was getting impatient. She decided to go ahead and show her pictures even though the women were still talking to each other.

"This set is from Miami," she cleared her throat and began. She handed the little plastic album to Charlotte. The women settled down. "We stayed the first night here and then got on the boat the following morning."

There were pictures of the desk clerk smiling, standing behind a tall wooden counter. A blue fish hung above her head. There were pictures of the lobby, wide and tropical with palm trees and tall, lacy ferns. There were shots of Dick unpacking in the room, the room service table with breakfast, Beatrice shopping for suntan lotion in the hotel sundries shop, and a couple of pictures of the bathtub, which was big enough for four people.

Charlotte then passed them on to Louise, who rolled her eyes. Here were twenty-four pictures of a hotel and the first night. It was going to be a long meeting. She finished and passed the album to Jessie, who passed it on to Margaret, sitting in the chair beside the sofa.

"Now these are from the boat before we sailed." Beatrice had been waiting for this opportunity for more than two weeks. She had taken two cameras, one that took wide-angle shots and the other, just a simple point-and-shoot. She was pleased with how the pictures had turned out and excited to share her photographic adventures.

"There are two different pictures of each shot." She proudly passed them to her pastor.

Charlotte turned quickly through the pages, passing them to Louise, who didn't even bother to look. She sat near Jessie so that it appeared they were seeing the photographs together.

There were pictures of people waving from the port up to the passengers on the ship, pictures of Dick and Beatrice arm in arm, pictures of seagulls and the pool and the ocean, and lots of shots of Dick studying things, the itinerary, the instruments on the front end of the ship, the menu in the dining room, and the list of costs of services. He seemed particularly engrossed in this piece of literature. His brow was crossed and he appeared to be chewing on his lip.

Beatrice rambled on as she handed the albums to Charlotte, who quickly flipped through the pictures and gave them to Louise.

"What are you doing here, Bea?" Jessie was more polite than Louise, trying to appear interested.

It was a photograph of Beatrice standing behind the captain, one hand waving to Dick, who was obviously taking the picture, and the other hand hidden behind the man's body. She had a strange smile on her face as she stood leaning against the side of the ship.

"Oh, that's Captain Mike. He was greeting the other passengers." She fumbled through the albums. "He had the cutest butt." She didn't look up as she went on. "I mean, the way his white jacket fell right at the rounded part. And his uniform pants were kind of tight." She motioned with her hands the line of the man's body. "It was real sexy, and Dick bet me that I wouldn't touch it."

Margaret looked at Jessie, surprised. But it was Louise who asked, as she pulled the album back towards her so that she could see the picture for herself, "You grabbed a man's ass?"

"Well, not grab exactly, just handled." Beatrice couldn't see why the women appeared so shocked.

Jessie and Margaret shook their heads. Charlotte got up from her seat to look over Louise's shoulder at the picture.

"Beatrice, you actually touched the captain's rear end?" After Charlotte sat back down, Jessie passed the album on to Margaret so that she could see the photograph for herself.

Beatrice sighed. She took a sip of her coffee and put down the cup. "I don't see what the fuss is all about. I handle dead people's butts all the time. And besides, there were a lot of folks around. I hardly think he figured out that I was intentionally rubbing him."

She saw no reason for this conversation and wished she had taken out that particular shot from the little album. She hadn't thought anyone else would notice that she wasn't just smiling and waving at the camera.

Jessie reached for a bit of her cake. "Girl, you are something."

"Beatrice, did the captain know you fondled him?" Charlotte couldn't believe what she was hearing.

"Beatrice, it doesn't look so crowded to me." Margaret was studying the picture. "Are you sure he didn't realize what you were doing?" She handed the album back to Beatrice, who had passed another one to Charlotte, who was waiting for the answer to Margaret's question.

She held the album in her hand, thinking, then replied, "Well, he did seem a little, oh, I don't know, nervous around me for the rest of the cruise."

She looked at the picture again, remembering the occasion. "We never got asked to sit at the captain's table for dinner."

Louise laughed.

"I just thought it was because Dick wore the same tie every night."

Jessie got up to get more coffee for everyone. "Beatrice, you cannot sit there and tell me you thought it was all right to touch another man's butt in public! I know you are not that naive."

She walked into the kitchen, then came back into the room.

Beatrice smiled and put the box of pictures down by her chair. She took a little more coffee from Jessie. "Oh, all right," she confessed, "I was a little nervous when I did it. But I did get a hundred dollars from Dick." She said this proudly. "And that counts for a lot because that man doesn't part with his money all that easy."

Louise sighed heavily and handed the next album to Jessie. She hadn't even looked at the pictures. She turned her attention to her friend sitting next to her. "So what's going on with you and the old man?" she asked.

"What do you mean?" Jessie replied. She was looking at the pictures from the second day of the cruise, and she was glad that Beatrice had quit passing more albums.

"I mean, why is he fixing up his car? He isn't leaving again, is he?"

Margaret turned so that she could see out the kitchen window into the backyard. James was standing on a crate, bending over the engine.

Jessie ate the rest of her cake. "He's got a leak," she replied hesitantly, "somewhere in the oil line."

No one said anything, and the room was quiet except for the clinking of forks on plates, cups on saucers. Louise simply stared at Jessie while she finished her dessert.

"What, Louise?" She pulled her body around so that she was facing the woman sitting next to her on the couch.

"I'm asking you what," Louise said.

The other women were silent.

Jessie took in a breath and held up the thermos with the coffee in it. It was a question if anyone wanted more. Everyone shook their heads. She poured herself another cup and stirred in the milk. Then she sat back on the sofa and began.

"James isn't sure he wants to stay here." She said this matter-of-factly, as if it were a weather report or the mention of some known event.

The women looked at each other, surprised at the comment, stunned at the news. James and

Jessie had been together again now for a number
of months, ever since their grandson's wedding.
They, like everyone else in the community and
the family, thought he was staying for good,
thought he had come home, landed safely back
in the cradle of his heart.

"What do you mean he doesn't want to stay
here?" Louise was angry. She had sat up on the
edge of her seat.

"He's bored. I don't know. He said he was
tired of the city, that he wanted to be back here,
in the country, with me. But I don't know; he's
just restless." Jessie stopped.

Margaret dropped her head. She knew what
this meant for Jessie.

"This place . . ." She stopped. "It's just got a
lot of bad memories for him."

Jessie got up, stacked up everyone's plates,
and walked with them into the kitchen. Still no
one spoke.

"So, take a trip," Beatrice offered cheerfully.
"It's amazing what a nice vacation can do for
your frame of mind. You can take a cruise or go
to the beach. Why don't you go on and retire

from that old mill you're still working at and the two of you take off for a couple of months somewhere?"

She put her napkin in her coffee cup and eased down in her chair. She thought it was a perfect solution. On their honeymoon, Dick had relaxed altogether into a different man. He was even considering selling the funeral home to one of the corporations that were starting to buy up all the family businesses. She was sure this was all James Senior needed.

Charlotte glanced up as Jessie walked back in the room. She sat back down in her seat. "Jessie, maybe that's not such a bad idea. Could you take some time together?"

Jessie smiled. "Well, funny you should mention that," she said as she threw her arm up over Louise. "I've decided to retire."

Louise nodded in approval and Margaret touched her on the leg. Charlotte let out a hooray and Beatrice clapped her hands lightly together.

"Good for you, Jessie," Margaret said. "You've been there a long time."

❧

"Lord yes, you've stayed with that mill family a whole lot longer than I was able to." Louise shifted so that she could look at Jessie without straining her neck. "And now they got the boy in charge. How do you put up with that snotty-nosed college boy as your boss?"

Jessie laughed. "Oh, he ain't so bad." She turned to Beatrice and said, "I just remind him that I'm someone who changed his diapers and whipped his butt."

Beatrice seemed pleased at this.

"And then he just backs out of my office and leaves me to do my work."

Margaret stacked the other photo albums on the coffee table and took her last bit of coffee. Then she wiped her mouth with her napkin. "That's just wonderful, Jessie. When's your last day?"

Before she could answer, James Senior walked in through the kitchen. He stopped at the door as the women were laughing and cheering.

"Well, what has made the committee so happy this evening?" He grinned at them and winked at Jessie.

Garden of Faith

"Jessie's just told us the big news that she's retiring." Charlotte spun around in her seat so that she could see James.

"Yes, and we're trying to decide where you should go in celebration," Beatrice added.

"Well, I guess she told you that we're planning to move out west." James did not realize the conversation hadn't gotten that far. "We're planning to celebrate the rest of our lives."

The room was still. Not one of the women moved in her seat or turned to look at Jessie. They just stayed that way, staring at James as he suddenly understood that they had not been told that part of the family's future plans.

Finally Margaret spoke. "Moving? Jessie, you're going to move?"

Jessie had not known how to tell her friends that she and James Senior were considering a move to California. She wasn't sure of what it would mean or how they would take it. She waffled between thinking that it wouldn't be a big deal, that they really weren't that close, and worrying that it would be more difficult to leave than she might imagine.

These women had become her family; and when James began to talk about moving, began pulling out pictures and books about northern California and the possibilities for them, she thought it was just a means to make her laugh. She merely played along with what she thought was only daydreaming. Then the conversations and the potential for moving became more real. And truthfully, she liked the thought of cleaning out her life, scaling down, and starting over in a new place. She found the idea exciting and began to let an old dream start to breathe.

She had loved it when she first left home for college. She loved learning a new city, meeting the new people, having the new experiences; and she never thought she would come back to Hope Springs. But Jessie soon learned that life rarely moves in the direction one first imagines for herself. And before she knew it, thirty years had come and gone and she was still only five miles from the place where her life began.

Before James's homecoming and before the spilling out of his old dreams, Jessie thought it was too late for her to think about a new move, a change, a new address. She figured she had aged out of the adventuresome life phases. She knew what her life was, and for the most part she was happy with it. She kept Hope and provided for Lana and Wallace while they were trying to get their feet off the ground. She didn't mind her work so much. She had other family close by. She had become settled; and she loved this group. These women. And there was this part, this surprising part—these women were harder for her to consider leaving than even her beloved grandchildren.

When Jessie began to make excuses about not being able to leave, James had not understood this, causing the biggest fight they had had since his return. He said that he could buy not wanting to leave family or a home; but four white women, one of them gay, another one just plain meddlesome, and another one younger than their children, well, this was simply beyond his comprehension. Margaret, he knew, was a good friend. She was reliable, sensible, and compassionate. But, he had told his wife, Margaret could visit often, stay as long as she liked. After all, he had added, she was alone, didn't have family; maybe she'd like to move with them. But the other three he had questioned: had they really gotten that close?

Jessie was mad at him for what he said; but she had stumbled on that. She had never had many friends growing up. She was always too busy to nurture relationships. With lots of chores to do at home, parents who maintained strict order, and her studious ways, there was very little time for a social life. When Jessie went to college, she met James early, so that any friends she had were always second priority to that primary relationship. It wasn't until now that she really felt as if she knew what it meant to have a friend. And she then realized that she had four. And these four were at least dear enough to have to give it a lot of thought before leaving them.

"Understand or not," she had told her husband in anger, "these women fill me up. It's going to take me a little time before I can just say good-bye and leave." And James had backed down, careful not to bring it up again.

Margaret was waiting for an answer. The other women now stared at her.

"Yes," she answered seriously, "James and I are planning to move to Oakland. He has a sister out there who'd like us to buy the place next to her." She moved around a bit, readjusting her position next to Louise.

"Jessie, how long have you been thinking about this?" Louise knew this was a question everyone had on their minds.

James left the room, quite sure that he was never going to hear the end of this from his wife. He walked out without anyone even noticing that he had gone.

"We started talking about it earlier this summer," Jessie said. "At first, I didn't think anything of it. But then, I don't know, I figured it would be fun." She tried to sound excited.

"When?" Charlotte just asked the one-word question.

"We don't know yet."

"Well, what are we talking about here?" Louise asked. "Fall, winter, next year?" She sounded angry.

"I don't know," Jessie said again.

Charlotte looked over to Margaret, wondering if she was going to tell her news as well. Margaret rubbed her hands up and down her legs and shook her head as an answer. Beatrice noticed the exchange and wondered what secret they shared.

"Well, I don't see how you could move before next year." Beatrice decided against asking Margaret what was going on and spoke to Jessie. "I mean, you have to retire, you'll have to clean out everything, you have to pack and get everybody settled. So that the earliest you could really leave is December, and you know you don't want to move in the cold."

Beatrice seemed to have it all figured out. At least if they knew it wasn't going to be anytime soon that Jessie was moving, they could clear the air of this heaviness and go back to looking at her albums.

"Did you see the pictures from when we went snorkeling?" She dropped to her side and picked up the box again.

"Beatrice, we don't want to see any more of your pictures. Frankly, the thought of seeing

Dick in a bathing suit is more than I can take right now." Louise tugged at the front of her shirt. "I can't believe you've been thinking about this for three months and not mentioned it to us." She was hurt at Jessie's silence.

The other women dropped their eyes. They felt the same way. Margaret, especially, felt a sense of betrayal that Jessie had not spoken of the possibilities. Hadn't they just been together last week at the mammogram? Why hadn't Jessie said anything then? And then she realized her own secret and figured that she had no room to make judgments.

"I'm sorry," Jessie said. "I was still trying to get used to the idea myself." She paused. "I like the idea of moving somewhere else. But it was hard thinking about telling anyone."

Charlotte didn't know what to say. She was as surprised and disappointed as the other women. Jessie was very dear to her. She was the voice of reason in the congregation, a person, like Margaret, that she knew would always find and tell the truth. She was solid, strong, and resilient. She held that community together; and Charlotte couldn't imagine being in the church without her.

"Well, I think this is horseshit." Louise was the only one not letting Jessie off the hook for her decision and her silence. And because these women knew Louise and loved her for who she was, even Jessie was not put off by her honesty. "You've been considering this the entire summer and you haven't let on, haven't asked us what we thought, haven't wanted our opinions. Well . . ." She stammered a bit. "I just think that's horseshit."

Still, the room was quiet.

Jessie turned to her friend sitting beside her. "Okay, Louise, tell me what you really think about me moving."

Louise didn't skip a beat. "I think it's horseshit. You let that man come back into your life after he walked out on you, and now you're just going to take up everything and follow him to California?" She was not to be stopped. "Suppose he gets bored out there, then what are you going to do?" She looked around for some help from Beatrice and Margaret, but they were silent.

"Horseshit," she said one more time.

"He's my husband, Louise. I love him. And I'm not doing this because he wants me to. Sure, it was his idea. But I very much like the idea. I've never wanted to stay here."

These words stung and the women looked as much.

Jessie realized how that sounded. "I don't mean it like that. I love you all. I love this house and my community. But I'm not at home here either. I like to travel. I've always thought I'd move somewhere else, but then there were the kids and Mama and Daddy to take care of. I want to experience life in another place before I die. I want to go with him. But I also want to go."

Even Beatrice felt a certain twinge of pain that friendship couldn't keep Jessie from making this decision. The women were left empty. The news sucked and drained them. They tried to appear understanding, tried even to look happy for their friend—everyone but Louise. She had decided that Jessie's choice was a choice against her, and she wanted nothing to do with being polite and gracious. She got up and started to leave.

"Well, I for one don't need to hear any more. This hurts me, Jessie, and I'll just have to be hurt for a little more before I can be nice."

She made an exit before anyone tried to stop her. They all four listened as Louise pulled out and drove away.

"Horseshit, huh?" Jessie asked the other women. "That what you think too?"

Margaret laughed slightly. "It's hard news to hear, Jes. You're like a sister to her, to all of us."

Jessie nodded without saying anything else.

"Well, look at the time!" Beatrice jumped up. "I have a husband of my own and he'll be waiting for me." She moved in front of Jessie. "I'll help you however I can." She reached out her hand. "And don't worry about Louise; she'll come around. I mean, she might not be pleasant, but she won't stay mad."

Jessie stood up and hugged Beatrice. "Don't forget your pictures."

"Oh, right." She went back to her seat and grabbed up the box. "Unless, does anyone want to keep them?"

Margaret and Charlotte both shook their

heads. Jessie threw up her hands before her, a negative gesture.

"Oh, okay. Then we meet next month at Margaret's, right?" She turned to Margaret.

Margaret nodded.

"All right then. I'll see everyone on Sunday." And she bounced out the door.

"I guess I should go too," Charlotte said as she got up from her seat. She set her coffee cup and saucer on the kitchen counter behind her. "I can't believe this, Jessie." This was all she could say. She hugged her friend and then looked at Margaret. "You coming?"

Margaret shook her head. "I want to talk a bit to Jessie."

Charlotte nodded and headed towards the door. She turned around and said, "Tell James I said goodnight."

"Yes," was Jessie's response. The young pastor left. She went to her car and sat down, but she did not leave.

Jessie began cleaning up. She wasn't sure what kind of reprimand she was about to get from her friend.

🌸

"Jessie, please, sit back down." Margaret remained in her seat.

"Margaret, I'm sorry. I should have told you," she said as she went back to the sofa. "I just . . ." She stammered a bit. "I just . . . it's just harder than I thought. I couldn't bring myself to tell you." She dabbed at her eyes with a tissue.

Margaret reached over and they held hands. "I know," she said.

There was a pause until they heard James moving things around in the back bedroom.

"That man!" Jessie said in exasperation. "His big mouth, and now if he wakes that baby!" She got up to leave, but Margaret held her hand tighter.

"Wait," Margaret said. "I have something I need to tell you too."

Charlotte watched through the window from her car as Margaret told the news to Jessie. She knew she shouldn't be spying like that, but she had been so curious about what Margaret was going to do. After the ultrasound and then the aspiration and hearing the doctor's recommendations, Margaret had decided to tell the group tonight. She was scheduled for surgery in two weeks.

The results could not be certain at this time. But the shape of the lump, the texture of the fluid, the results from the blood test from her earlier appointment all seemed to point to cancer. Although they could move more conservatively and just do a biopsy, the radiologist, the surgeon, and her doctor concurred that a lumpectomy was really the safest way to go. They believed that the tumor was small and contained and were hopeful that with its early detection and removal, they could isolate and eliminate any more signs of the disease. They had all agreed this was the best route to take.

Charlotte had sat in the room with Margaret as all the reports were read. She reached for and held Margaret's hand at one point. But she felt incomplete, fragmented; and she had told Margaret so. "The others should have been with us," she had said to Margaret, who had nodded in agreement. And they both decided at that point that, for the rest of the way, Margaret would let the other women be a part of the process.

Jessie sat back at first and then dropped to her knees in front of Margaret. Then she pulled her out of her own chair and into herself, and they stayed like that for a very long time.

Charlotte folded her arms around the steering wheel. She wept while she watched two women, two friends, fall into each other and into the sadness and into the fear and the sorrow. She saw them rock and sit back and wipe the tears and hold each other some more.

It was powerful, she thought, what women bring to each other in calamity. It may not be forceful or disciplined or organized. It may not solve anything or provide a linear direction for others to follow. It may not have the intensity or action that men's responses often have. On the surface it might even appear sparse or meager, insignificant, small. Many will pass right over it, never even recognizing its strength. But Charlotte knew it to be what it was. It was the place from which everything else grew. It was rich and fertile, the foundation of life. It was the bedrock of faith.

The young pastor started the car and pulled out into the night.

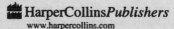

Rita Award-winning author

Georgia Bockoven

"Bockoven is magic."
New York Times bestselling author Catherine Coulter

ANOTHER SUMMER
0-380-81865-5/$6.99 US/$9.99 Can
"*Another Summer* is Georgia Bockoven at her very best.
Heartbreaking and uplifting, poignant and triumphant . . .
it will appeal to anyone who believes
in the healing power of love."
Kristin Hannah

Also by the author

THE BEACH HOUSE
0-06-108440-9/$6.50 US/$8.50 Can

DISGUISED BLESSING
0-06-103020-1/$6.50 US/$8.99 Can